"Okay, so how am I supposed to act at school?" Howie asked.

"Always listen, and do your homework." Al handed Howie a computerized list of do's and don'ts. "And be polite to Mrs. Blesinger," he warned.

"Now I'll pretend to be Mrs. B.," Al said. He put on one of Mom's scarves and spoke in a falsetto voice. "Good morning, Howie. I see you're new here. Where are you from?"

"I'm from Timmy's basement, California and Japan," Howie said.

"Howie!" I yelled. "Don't tell her *that!*"

"But yesterday you explicitly told me I was put together in the basement."

"Mrs. B. will think you're a weirdo," Al said.

"Why?" Howie asked. "I'll just explain that I'm an android . . ."

HIGH-TECH HOWARD

#1
My Cousin the Droid
Max Taylor

PRICE STERN SLOAN
Los Angeles

Produced by Cloverdale Press, Inc.
96 Morton Street
New York, New York 10014

Published by Price Stern Sloan, Inc.
360 North La Cienega Boulevard
Los Angeles, California 90048

ISBN 0-8431-2712-0

10 9 8 7 6 5 4 3 2 1

ONE

If you ask me, my family is the weirdest one in America. Or maybe they're the weirdest in the world.

Take my parents, for instance. They look and act as if they were freeze-dried in the sixties. My mom wears a peace symbol necklace, likes dresses made from India-print bedspreads, and she never cuts her hair. My Dad is no better. His red hair is long and frizzy and he drives a fluorescent painted van. They are both physics professors at Chicago City University. I bet that no other place would hire anyone who looks like them.

Then there's my fifteen-year-old brother, Albert "Einstein" Watkins, the incredible math and science whiz. His IQ is so high it's off the charts, and the two of us are complete opposites.

Al loves school and skipped two grades. He'll graduate early, and colleges are already begging him to accept scholarships.

I thrive on football, baseball and multiple-choice tests. I spent summer vacation practicing passes and kicks with my team, the Sixth Grade Wolverines, so we can smash the Seventh Grade Samurais, in the annual challenge game when school starts.

But Albert spent every day of his vacation in the basement building Project H—or Howie Pentergasser—the most advanced computerized android known to man, or so Al says. Howie looks so human that there's a slight resemblance between the two of us. People will actually think he's my cousin. Except for my family, nobody can ever know that Howie is really a computer. It's top secret. Otherwise people might think that Al is so geeky, he'd prefer an android to a real live friend.

Howie has already been registered as a new student at Clifton Elementary; he'll be in Mrs. Blesinger's sixth-grade room with me.

"You mean you're building a new little brother because I'm not smart enough for you?" I asked Al when he first drew up plans for Howie and began testing hard disks and circuit boards.

"Don't be so sensitive, Timmy," Al answered, peering at me through his thick glasses. "I'm programming him to play every game you've ever heard of—and some even you don't know about."

"You mean he'll be able to play baseball and football?" I asked excitedly. My parents and brother are so into scientific theory that they barely realize sports exist.

"Yes, Timmy," Al said in a condescending tone. "Howie will be an integration of both of our strong points. My unusually high-level intellectual gifts will be incorporated with your typical American sports knowledge and pre-adolescent social skills."

"Yeah," I answered. Al's attitude annoyed me. "Maybe somebody in this house will finally be able to play ball with me! And don't call me Timmy. My name is Tim."

"Tim, Timothy or Timmy. It's all the same, little brother," Al muttered as he tested the speech adapter that would make Howie talk.

I hate the way I get no respect around here just because I'm the youngest, and the family's scientific brain cell pool ran out when Al was born. Believe you me, I'm no dummy. I'm captain of the Sixth Grade Wolverines and their fullback. It takes plenty of intelligence to figure out good plays and to make sure everybody on the team gets along.

Al's attitude aggravated me less as I thought about Project H's possible good points. Howie might not be ready in time to practice football, but he could play ice hockey and basketball later. And, best of all, maybe he could do my math and science homework, as long as nobody else found out.

Finally, the day before school started, Howie was ready to be turned on to meet his new family. My folks had proudly agreed to pose as Howie's Uncle Peter and Aunt Marcy. Supposedly, Howie's folks were also slightly eccentric professors, who had left their son at our place while studying environmental ozone in various locations around the world. Unfortunately, Al's schedule for Howie's completion was about a month behind because of faulty circuit-board wires and a minor programming glitch. We were kind of worried that we wouldn't have enough time to teach Howie how to behave around teachers and the kids at school.

To make things comfortable for Howie's awakening, we put him on the other twin bed in my bedroom, since he'd be sleeping there and hanging out with me. His body gave me an eerie feeling. He wasn't switched on yet and didn't display a breathing motion, so he reminded me of a corpse.

"Wait till you see the outfit I got him," Al said. He dumped out some clothes from a bag.

I'd expected Al to have a pair of jeans and some kind of cool jersey for Howie. But Al's selections were geek city. The outfit consisted of brown polyester dress pants and a hideous orange plaid sport coat.

"Are you out of your mind?" I asked him. "No self-respecting android would be caught turned on *or* off in this!"

"C'mon, Timmy, I want Howie to look nice for the first day of school."

"Don't call me that dumb Timmy name. I've reminded you a zillion times," I said angrily.

Albert let out an exasperated sigh. "Okay, *Tim*, I want Howie to make a good impression. You know how Mrs. Blesinger is."

"I know exactly how she is. Nauseating! She'll expect me to be just like you, making A's in everything except phys. ed. and citizenship."

Al rolled his eyes. "Don't be so juvenile. I can't help it if I'm the best student she's ever had."

"Think about the other kids in school, Al. Howie won't last until lunchtime if he goes dressed like a forty-year-old man." I tossed my favorite Cubs T-shirt and a pair of faded jeans by Howie's bed. "Put these on him."

Albert stared at me. "I will not have my creation showing up at school dressed like a slob!" he argued.

"Oh, yeah? Well, I'll pretend I don't know him if he wears those creepy clothes you just bought."

"I spent two months' allowance on them!" Al said. "He's going to wear them whether you like it or not." He lifted Howie up off the bed and started to put the polyester pants on him.

I tried to stop him, and Al shoved me. Then I punched Al and he socked me back—hard. For a nerd, Al can be pretty strong sometimes. The two of us started wrestling with each other on the bedroom floor.

"Boys! What are you two arguing about now?" My mother rushed upstairs from the kitchen, where she was busily preparing organic eggplant casserole, marinated alfalfa salad, and carob cake for Howie's coming-out lunch.

My father followed. He looked annoyed, since we had obviously interrupted his meditation hour. "You both know that fighting, in any form, is not allowed in this house."

"Al bought Howie a geek suit to wear to school tomorrow," I complained. "And he tried to clobber me when I gave Howie a decent outfit to wear."

"I invented him," Al protested. "I should at least be able to choose his duds for the first day of school."

"If he's going to hang around with me, I want him to look like my friends—not a dork!"

"Don't call your brother names, Timothy Watkins." My mother frowned. "Your brilliant brother has a brilliant scientific experiment here, a human clone that might be an ambassador for world peace."

"It won't be very peaceful for Howie," I told my family, "if he shows up at school in that stuff."

My father rubbed his love beads. "But I think perhaps the best solution would be to let Howie choose his own outfit, as soon as he's booted up."

My folks quickly went back downstairs. They instinctively knew that an eleven-year-old boy—even if he was a computerized replica—would not want to get dressed in front of them.

A few moments later, Al pressed numerous buttons on a remote-control box and announced proudly, "Our new cousin, Howie Pentergasser, will now come to life."

Immediately bleeps, yawns and sighs came out of Howie. He stretched and looked at the alarm clock. "Hey, I overslept," he said.

"Wow!" I shouted. "He's for real!"

Al and I both jumped up and down, hugged each other and shook hands.

"I knew it would work! I knew it would work!" Al congratulated himself.

"Incredible." I waved my fists in the air. Too bad I couldn't brag to the guys—that I was the only kid in history who had a custom-made friend.

Howie eyed us with a mixture of curiosity and boredom, then he tapped me on the shoulder. "I'd like to ask you a favor."

"Sure, Howie," I answered. It was hard to believe that I was actually talking to a robot.

He looked at my Chicago Bears posters on the wall disdainfully. "I'd appreciate it if you'd exchange these wall decorations. I like the Los Angeles Rams."

"The Bears are better," I told him.

"That's a matter of opinion," Howie answered, and proceeded to examine the two selections of clothing. "You don't expect me to wear those monkey clothes in public, do you?" He made a face at Al's choices and stuck out his tongue.

Except for the fact that Howie preferred the Rams to the Chicago Bears, I liked him already.

Both Al and I watched in amazement as Howie pulled on my jeans, threw down the

Cubs shirt and took a plain yellow polo top from my drawer. "I like the Dodgers, not the Cubs," Howie informed us.

"How come you're so hung up on California?" I asked.

"Because," Howie answered, "I was born there."

"You were not," Al corrected him, and looked at him in surprise. "You were created by trial and error, in the basement of this house."

"Maybe so." Howie walked around the room taking everything in. "But my circuit boards, hard disks and programs were all made in California, except for the chips that came from Japan. I'm from California, so there."

"I suppose you do have a point," Al answered. We both watched Howie pace around the room.

Howie strode over to my closet and checked my sports equipment out. "Nice catcher's mitt. Hey, where did you get this baseball autographed by Don Rensinger?"

"Our Little League team won the Midwest championships, and Don sent an autographed ball to each of us," I said.

Howie examined the rest of my stuff without further questions until he came to my lace-up roller skates. "What are these? A pair

9

of motorized camping boots?'' 'A bewildered look crossed Howie's face.

"No. It's a pair of skates," I said, and demonstrated.

"Out of sight! Let me try! I want to walk on wheels.'' Howie excitedly put on the skates.

"Careful. They go real fast,'' I warned him.

"Don't worry.'' Howie sounded confident. Then he wobbled and whizzed across the room for a moment, before crashing to the floor with a loud thud.

"Omigod! Howie broke already, and it's my fault,'' I said in disbelief.

Both Al and I rushed over to Howie. We poked and shook him . . . and looked at each other in panic.

"Howie, please get it together.'' Al put his ear to the android's chest. The only sound that came out of Howie was a slight mechanical buzz.

Then, a second later, when the phone in the upstairs hallway rang, Howie jumped up and made a dash for it on the roller skates.

"Fooled you!'' Howie laughed. "I can even play dead. Watkins residence,'' he said in a serious voice as he answered the phone.

"Don't do that again,'' Al scolded Howie.

"He's great,'' I told Al. "He'll certainly liven up things at school.''

"Ms. Susi Weiland for Mr. Timothy Watkins." Howie smirked and handed the phone to me. "I didn't know you had a girl friend."

I scowled at him and covered the receiver with my hand. "She's not my girl friend. Susi Weiland is the manager of the Wolverines, and she does a good job."

Howie pantomimed the act of kissing and hugging a girl. But Susi really isn't a typical girl. She knows everything about football, and has even thought of some winning strategies herself. But one thing about her that disgusts me is the way she shrieks when she gets upset or excited—which she was definitely doing now.

"Something horrible has happened!" Her high voice sounded unusually irritating over the phone, and I held it away from my ear.

"What is it?" I asked.

"Remember how Crusher Callahan's dad got transferred to the Milwaukee office of his company a few weeks ago? Well, they found a house up there, and the whole family moved yesterday!" she announced.

"They *what*?" I asked in horror. Crusher, whose real name is Kelly Callahan, is the biggest and fastest kid at Clifton Elementary. He's probably the biggest sixth-grader in existence, our star quarterback, and the key to our team's success. Without Crusher, we could easily end up losing the big challenge game and be forced to spend the first month of school washing the seventh-graders' lockers.

"What should we do?" I asked her. For a second I considered the possibility of using Howie on the team. But I wasn't quite sure about him after the incident on the skates.

"Let's have a special meeting tonight," she answered. "Coach Rumbaugh thinks that with enough surprise plays we'll beat them even without Killer. By the way, who answered the phone?" she asked. "It didn't sound like your brother."

"That's my cousin Howie from California. He'll be living here for the year. He's cute," I teased Susi. One of my plans for Howie was to get some girl to have a crush on him—a snob like Melinda Peavy. Melinda wears designer clothes and perfume to school.

"I don't care if he's cute or not," Susi answered sharply. "What I want to know is, has he ever played on a good football team?"

"Hold on a second." I stuck my head into the bedroom. "Hey, Howie! Have you ever played football?"

Howie pretended to be catching a pass and ran around the room. I was glad to see that he had taken off my roller skates before he really got hurt. "I played for the Racing Robots. I can be programmed to do anything," Howie said.

"I'll bring Howie to the meeting tonight," I told Susi. "He'll be a terrific quarterback." At least, that's what I hoped!

"Quarterback? I don't want to be part of something." Howie looked disappointed. "I want to be a whole back, or I won't play."

"I'll talk to you later, Susi." I hung up the phone quickly and glared at my brother. "I thought you programmed Howie to play sports. He doesn't even know what the positions are."

"Football, football!" Howie hollered. He put on my helmet, threw my football into the air, and bashed it across the room, using my tennis racket for a bat. He almost broke the lamp by my bed.

"Maybe something got mixed up with the circuits." Al looked perplexed. "Or maybe the box that holds the sports memory loosened when he fell."

Al switched off Howie, and together we carried him into the basement.

"Don't worry, he'll be in shape for tonight," Al promised me.

Somehow, I wasn't so sure.

TWO

"I may as well show you how Project H works now." Al unlocked the door to the basement workshop, and I switched on the light.

I tried hard not to jolt Howie. We both placed him carefully on a thickly padded work table. I sure didn't want to damage anything else inside him and have him act worse than before. I'd never live it down if Howie started acting weird around my friends.

I looked around the workshop for a minute. I didn't understand why it had to be top secret all summer. It appeared to be a general hobby-room setup. There was a computer desk on one end of the room, and on the other side lay tools and a conglomeration of electronic parts.

Al pulled up Howie's shirt and ran a finger along a huge scar on the right side of Howie's waist.

"What happened to him?" I asked Al. It looked like a dog had attacked him, or maybe he had had his appendix out.

But Al ignored me and started to jab Howie's skin.

"Hey, what are you doing to him?" I winced and yanked Al's arm away from Howie. Things I hate include pain, guts and anything gory. The way Al had been poking at Howie, I figured he'd hurt him. I sure didn't want Howie bleeding all over the floor.

"Calm down," Al said. "I'm not hurting him. When Howie is turned off, he can't feel a thing."

I breathed a sigh of relief. Although I'd only known Howie for only an hour, it was hard not to think he wasn't a real person.

"I'm glad you reacted so strongly, though," Al added. "I couldn't think of a better location for the battery chamber. By designing the skin to look like a scar, nobody will get suspicious when you guys dress for gym."

"Very clever," I told Al. "You really had me going."

Al flipped up the skin, and I peered at Howie's insides, remembering last year's health class on the human body. Instead of veins and intestines, Howie's body was filled with wires, chips and electronic equipment.

And Howie could eat like a regular person. Al had installed a trash compactor into Howie, where the digestive system normally is.

Al clicked open the black metal box that housed Howie's batteries. "Now there are four batteries that control the operating system. If one goes out, Howie will nod his head like he's sleepy."

Personally, I thought that was poor planning. "What do I do when that happens? If he starts sawing Zs at school, Mrs. Blesinger will march him down to the principal's office for sure."

"You pretend you both go to the bathroom and replace it. Or if there isn't a bathroom or some other place private, you'll have to go home. We can't risk people questioning us." Al handed me two packs of batteries. "Make sure that whenever you're with Howie you have a spare set."

"You mean he's going to need replacements all the time?" I asked.

"About once a week," Al answered.

For the next few minutes I practiced removing and replacing batteries. They had to be placed precisely, or the whole system could be messed up.

17

Then Al showed me how to use the automatic component for switching Howie on and off. It worked like a remote control on a TV set, and needed to be aimed straight at Howie to work correctly.

"Never abuse your ability to control Howard. The box should only be used for extreme situations, like upstairs," Al warned me. "Howie should be allowed to misbehave like any other sixth-grade kid."

Al explained that Howie had a central processor in his head similar to a human brain. The processor had an intricate disk operating system that controlled all of Howie's activities, using numerous sets of software. Howie could even speak Spanish and French.

"I'd like you to check the sports program over, Tim," Al said, holding Howie's sports disk up to the light.

I turned on Al's computer and popped the disk in, expecting it to be full of misinformation. But when I looked at the data on the screen, everything was one hundred percent correct. Al had typed in every player's position with a detailed description, names of well-known players and examples of their winning plays. He'd included an appendix of football history and a directory of rules.

"Is everything I typed in accurate?" Al asked.

"Wow! How did you know all this?" I slapped Al on the back.

Al opened up a cabinet above the worktable, filled with sports guides of every description. Al hadn't been exaggerating when he told me Howie would be programmed with games I didn't know about. The collection included manuals on cricket, rugby and squash.

"Hey, you want to go to a football game with me sometime?" I asked.

"You better believe it," Al answered. "I'd come to this evening's practice, but it might look suspicious. I promise I'll be at that annual challenge game, though."

"You mean it? Do you think Mom and Dad will go?" I asked.

"I've already talked to them about coming, and they'll be there, too," Al said.

This was a change for the better. My folks always go to Al's science exhibits, but they rarely come to watch me play sports. They especially hate football, because they think it's a violent way for me to express myself. Sometimes I think they're ashamed that I don't have Al's academic skills, and wish that they had a different younger son.

Al tightened some wires on Howie, and an amused look crossed his face. "I've got everything so well programmed in Howie, he'll knock everybody's kneepads off at practice." Al stuck the sports diskette back into Howie and booted him up again.

"Hey, where am I?" Howie demanded. "And what did you two guys do to me before?"

"Something got messed up and we had to repair you," I told him. "So you got shut off."

"Well, don't do it again without warning me," Howie said.

"I wouldn't have, but you were acting insane." I figured I better test him on football, just to be safe. "What's a quarterback?" I asked.

"The quarterback is the most active player on the offensive team. No matter what happens on the field, the quarterback orders the play and takes action. A quarterback must be alert, respected and a good leader." Howie brightened. "Boy, would I like that spot!"

"You have a good chance of getting it, since you know me," I said. "I'm the captain, so the other kids pretty much listen to me. But you'll have to show the coach you're a good player," I told him, "or you'll never make the team."

"Don't worry about my athletic abilities," Howie said.

Both Al and Howie smiled as if there was a secret between them.

"Now, listen closely." I began explaining the evening's activities. "We're going over to Potowatamie Field later for an important football meeting, so you've got to be on your best behavior."

"Sure." Howie smirked, looked at me cross-eyed and emitted a few musical bleeps.

"Howie, no bleeping or playing dead like before!" Al ordered.

"You guys aren't much fun, are you?" Howie bleeped again. "I'm glad I'm an android, and not a person." Then he started humming a computerized version of "Take Me Out to the Ball Game."

"Howie, I mean it! First of all, you can't go around telling people you're a robot. You've got to act human at all times," Al said sternly.

Howie frowned. "But I'm proud of my electronic heritage. I shouldn't have to hide it from anyone. Everybody knows you and Al are human, don't they?"

"That's different," I told him. "All people are humans."

"And all androids are robots," Howie answered sarcastically. "I can tell anybody I want."

"Oh no, you can't. If anybody finds out you're an android, every newspaper and TV station in America will send a reporter to our house. That's why nobody can know the truth about you," I said.

"So," answered Howie. "What's wrong with a little publicity?" He grabbed a surge protector bar and held it up in front of his face like a microphone. "Hello, America. In a Chicago suburb today, the hobby of human cloning was given new meaning. . . ."

"You would *not* want publicity," Al interrupted Howie. He pointed to a huge box under the workbench. "If you utter even a syllable about being an android, we're all doomed—especially you."

"Doomed?" asked Howie. "Why's that?"

"Because." Al continued pointing to the box of discarded computer parts under the workbench. "Somebody would probably kidnap you, and you'd end up looking like that."

Howie gulped and started to act more serious. "So, uh, how should I act around your football team?"

I thought it over for a moment. It's not easy to tell somebody else—especially an android—how to behave around your friends. "Just act cool, but don't be a wise guy."

Howie looked thoughtful.

"And," Al added, "these kids are very serious about playing football—don't take the games lightly. Last year the losers spit in the winners' hands instead of shaking them.'' Al glanced at me.

I blushed. Al was referring to the fifth-grade–sixth grade game the year before. I hadn't thought up the spitting idea, but I'd gone along with it. Now, as a sixth-grader, it seemed incredibly childish.

Howie repeated our advice and pretended to write it on the palm of his hand. ''No telling anybody I'm a robot, no spitting, no bleeping. Can I laugh and breathe?'' he asked.

''No acting sarcastic, either,'' I warned him.

''Time to eat!'' my mother called from the top of the stairway.

We all ran upstairs. After my folks were introduced to Howie, they hugged him and wished him good karma.

To celebrate the occasion, my father read a poem before lunch, and my mother strummed along on her guitar. Then we all toasted Howie with glasses of homemade carrot juice.

Howie kicked me under the table to let me know he thought my folks were acting ridiculous. I was glad he agreed with me. Now I'd have a kid my age who understood how embarrassing my parents were.

''Now, what are your plans for the rest of

the day?" my mother asked while passing tofu appetizers around.

"Howie and I are going to practice passing this afternoon, and then we'll both go practice with the team tonight," I said.

"What?" my father asked, as if I had told him I planned to take Howie's batteries out and toss him down a sewer.

"It's a good way for him to meet the guys," I argued. "I think Howie will make a great quarterback, and we need a replacement now that Crusher Callahan moved."

"Oh, I'm so glad," my mother said. She sounded elated. "I never liked that Callahan boy. His parents staunchly supported the war when we were in college. You can never trust people like that."

"Marcy," my father interrupted. "We can't hold grudges over things in the past. The main problem I have is that our dear robotic nephew may overheat by playing outdoors. It could ruin his hard-disk subsystem, and all of Albert's hard work will be for nothing.

"But Al designed him to be athletic," I reminded him. "And you can't play anything but table tennis inside!"

"Timmy," my father told me, "you have no idea what goes into robotics. What Howie does every day is not up to you."

"I thought you wanted me to be good friends with Howie and have stuff in common with him," I said.

"I want to go to practice with Tim," Howie stated firmly.

"He's not going," my father answered flatly.

Then we started screaming and yelling at each another. Howie just watched us with a curious stare.

"Hold it! Hold it!" Al yelled, trying to calm us down. "I've devised everything to hold up under different weather conditions, including high temperatures. Howie just can't stay out too long in the rain. I'm already working on a waterproof backup system for that."

After lunch, Al and I made Howie practice running, kicking and catching balls—although Al is so uncoordinated that he wasn't much help. But I could see now what he'd meant about Howie knocking the other team's kneepads off. I'd never seen anyone run so fast in my life.

"Do you feel okay?" I asked Howie when he slowed down a little.

"I feel a little wasted. I'm not used to so much happening in one day. It's pretty tough to be born at age eleven, you know," Howie said.

"He doesn't need a new battery change,

does he?'' I asked Al. I felt like I was talking about a baby and his diapers!

''No, not unless he's yawning or nodding his head,'' Al said.

''But he says he's worn out,'' I told Al.

''He has to act human or he wouldn't be a state-of-the-art android. Don't *you* get tired when you work out?'' Al asked.

''Of course,'' I answered. Usually after a game or practice I chug down a couple of glasses of soda before collapsing in front of the TV set. Sometimes the whole team stops for a snack at Frankie's Fast Food. It's got twenty-five flavors of ice-cream sodas and a dessert bar.

''Howie isn't much different than you,'' Al explained. ''He gets tired, too.''

After we were finished with our backyard practice, I showed Howie our playbook.

''I think we can do better than that,'' he told me. ''The Wolverines will win this game easily.''

''You mean it, Howie?''

''I'll devise some intricate plays,'' Howie assured me. ''I'll know more after tonight's practice.''

As we walked over to the field that evening, I hoped he was right.

THREE

"So, you think Howard here is going to make up for Crusher?" Coach Rumbaugh looked over Howie carefully, the way my mom does when she's deciding to buy a piece of furniture at the thrift shop downtown.

None of the other kids had arrived at the field yet. I'd brought Howie a little early so I could introduce him to the coach and show him around.

"Howie will be terrific," I assured him. "He's alert, he can think quickly and he's a fast runner. I showed him our playbook and taught him the signals. He's definitely the right . . . uh, guy for the job."

"I don't know," Coach Rumbaugh mused. "I know you're the captain, Watkins, and Howie is your cousin, but I think Jennifer El-

27

lison would make a good quarterback. She's been playing football since third grade, she's an outstanding player and all the guys respect her. I'd like to see her as quarterback myself."

"Aw, come on, Coach! You don't want some girl playing the most important position. The seventh-graders will give us an extra-bad time then," I told him.

Howie stood there quietly, smiling now and then—just like I hoped he would. Neil Langford, our center, arrived, and Howie did a fairly decent job of introducing himself.

"Howie, why don't you tell me where you played ball," the coach asked.

Howie grinned. "I played for the Racing—"

I threw Howie a look and cleared my throat loudly.

"The Racing Rangers, at Lomand Elementary in Fullerton, California." Howie grinned again. "We had a junior league that started in third grade. I played guard, halfback and safety. My last year there I was quarterback."

"Fullerton?" Coach sounded excited. "Do you know Mike Shipton? He's an old buddy of mine from college. I think he's principal at one of the elementary schools there."

"Which one?" Howie asked, sounding interested.

I could tell Howie was getting a kick out of putting the coach on, but if he kept it up he'd get himself into deep trouble.

"Uh, Howie went to a private school," I interrupted.

"What's your last name, Howie?"

"Pentergasser. My folks live on Strawberry Lane."

"I wonder if that's near where Skip lives. . . . Maybe he knows your folks. Next time I write to him I'll ask him if he knows the Pentergassers," Coach Rumbaugh promised.

"Howie's folks are traveling professors and kind of different . . . like my folks," I said.

Coach Rumbaugh stared at me blankly. He doesn't think much of my parents. Mr. Rumbaugh was my third-grade teacher, and he had a huge argument with my mother when we learned about the western expansion. Mom wrote up her own lesson on how rotten the settlers were to the Indians, and asked me to give it to him. Needless to say, Coach Rumbaugh did not appreciate being told how to teach his class.

Howie and the coach continued discussing the virtues of California while I watched Howie carefully out of the corner of my eye.

I told each player about Howie as they showed up. There are seventeen members on the Wolverines, nine who'll be in Mrs. Blesinger's class and eight who'll have Miss Lavery when school starts. Two of our players are female. Jennifer Ellison plays left halfback and cornerback. I've got to admit that Jennifer is fast and carries the ball well. But the other girl, Fran Wallin, is terrible. She only made the team because she's big and is good at knocking people down. Because we're short on players, some team members play both offense and defense.

"So, what's the story?" I asked when Howie was through talking with the coach.

"He wants to see how well I run and throw passes today. I guess we're going to play something called touchy football since I don't have any equipment yet."

"Howie, it's called *touch* football," I told him. "That means we touch other team members to stop them, instead of actually tackling them. And be careful. Some of the kids get really rough around here. They play for blood, even in practice."

Howie smiled at me. "They really pull out your wires, huh?"

The two of us walked over to the fence where everybody usually stands before practice, and I introduced him to the rest of the team.

Everyone was pretty nice, except for Jennifer. She probably knew she could be passed over for quarterback because of him.

I caught a glimpse of Susi and the coach nodding their heads and pointing to Jennifer and Howie, as though they were discussing them. I also noticed Ron Mason, the eighth-grader who does the "Kidbits" column for the local paper, watching us. He roams around various school events looking for exciting stories. Personally, I doubted that our practice rated as something to write about.

Howie seemed to be observing everything, including the cheerleaders as they pranced into the park. They weren't in uniform, but they were waving their red-and-white pompons.

"Hey, what are those girls with the colored mops doing?" Howie whispered in my ear.

"Those are not colored mops, they're pompons. And the girls are called cheerleaders. They shake the pompons during their routines to boost everyone's team spirit."

"They look pretty cheerful," Howie joked, and pointed to Sharon Rawson, the head cheerleader, and Melinda Peavy, who were headed our way. Sharon looked especially pretty. When she got closer and smiled, I noticed that sometime over the summer she'd had her braces taken off and had cut and curled her hair.

I don't like Melinda, but I do like Sharon. I've had a crush on her ever since she gave me a glow-in-the-dark pen at the fourth-grade Christmas gift exchange.

"You're new, aren't you?" Melinda gave Howie the once-over. "I'm Melinda," she introduced herself.

"I'm Sharon Rawson." Sharon extended her hand toward Howie. "Welcome to the neighborhood."

"Glad to meet you." Howie took Sharon's hand and shook it politely.

"Time to play ball!" Coach Rumbaugh shouted, and his whistle shrieked.

We all dashed out onto the field.

As usual, the coach barked his pre-practice orders. "Number seventeen!" he shouted to Noah Morse, our center. "Get that uniform washed by tomorrow or don't show up. And, you, Josh Peterson, I want that gum out of your mouth. Now, Wieland wants to make an announcement," Coach said.

Susi sauntered up in front of the team with her clipboard. "Some of you may not know yet, but Crusher Callahan has moved out of town. Since we need somebody to replace him, Coach and I have decided to try out both

Ellison and Pentergasser. In case you haven't met Pentergasser, he's Watkins's cousin." Susi pointed to Howie.

Howie gave the other guys the thumbs-up sign.

Because I'm the captain and Howie's my cousin, all the guys started yelling "Power to Pentergasser!" when Howie presented himself. They booed when Susi mentioned Jennifer's name.

"Don't forget your sportsmanship!" Coach Rumbaugh shouted. He frowned at all of us. "Give Ellison a chance."

"But, coach," Josh Peterson complained. "It's hard enough to have a girl for our manager. Quarterback is out of the question."

"Yeah? Well, I'll walk if she doesn't get it," Noah threatened. "I don't think a total stranger should be considered just because he's the captain's cousin. That's lousy, if you ask me."

"Team!" the coach shouted. "Do I have to remind you about sportsmanship again? If we're not together as a team, we'll *give* the game to the Samurai because we're a bunch of babies who can't work our differences out. You want that to happen?"

Everybody yelled "No way!"

"All right then," Coach Rumbaugh said.

"Let's get to work." He pulled Susi and me into a huddle.

"What I want to do," Coach informed us, "is try both of them out on basic skills, and then watch Howie play."

"We should probably check them out for speed—have them run the fifty-yard dash," I suggested. "Then see how they do on distance throwing."

"What about blocking and tackling?" Susi asked.

"That's very important here," Coach agreed. "We need a strong defense, too."

I remembered what had happened that morning when Howie fell over skating. "Uh, in all fairness I don't think we should do that, Coach. Jennifer isn't such a great tackle and she'd be at a disadvantage," I said, thinking quickly. Besides, I was afraid of what it would feel like to be tackled by a computer.

"Okay," the coach agreed.

Somehow, though, I felt both Susi and the coach wanted Jennifer to get the job.

"First we'll try them out on the dash with the ball." Susi pointed to a spot on the fifty-yard line and tossed Jennifer the ball. Then she looked at her stopwatch and shouted, "Go!"

Jennifer ran the dash in 7.0 seconds, which borders on excellent, but Howie ran it in 5.5.

"Amazing!" Coach Rumbaugh said. "I want this kid on the baseball team and the track team. He doesn't run, he flies."

Jennifer couldn't get anywhere close to Howie on the catching or the passing. Howie could throw the ball accurately for more than sixty yards. He punted like somebody already in high school. I didn't need to worry about anybody knocking Howie over, because nobody could catch up with him.

After practice everybody shook Howie's hands, and about a dozen team members lifted Howie on their shoulders.

"Boy, they really train them out in California," Josh said before walking over to the area by the stands. For a moment, Noah spoke with Sharon Rawson and the rest of the cheerleading squad.

A few minutes later, the girls turned toward Howie and waved their pompons.

"Howie, Howie, H-o-w-i-e. He might be new to Clifton, but he'll win the game for me!"

"What a practice," Neil Langford said. "Let's hit Frankie's!"

While some of the other kids changed clothes in the park house, Howie observed the seventh-graders finishing up their practice on the other side of the field.

"What do you think?" I asked.

"They're a little bigger than us, but slightly clumsy. I'll process some tactics by tomorrow. They have a rather disorganized offense," he concluded.

A few seconds later, Ron Mason, the reporter, came over to Howie and me. "Hey, kid, are you going to school here?" he asked.

"Yeah," Howie answered. "For the year, anyway."

"You really played well at practice. What's your name?"

Howard smiled. "You can call me Howie."

"His entire name is Howard Pentergasser," I interrupted.

Ron jotted down a few things. "Are you going to be at the game this Sunday?"

"Of course! I'm the quarterback," Howie said.

"Really? What about Callahan? Was he kicked off the team?"

"No," I told him, "he moved."

"Very interesting," Ron said before walking away.

When we arrived at Frankie's, the place was packed. It's not the sort of place where somebody seats you. If it's crowded, you wait and then make a mad dash for an empty table. A family with about ten little kids was sitting at the big table by the window that we usually use.

"Hey," Howie said, "there's a place!" He strode toward a big table in the back.

I rushed after him and pulled him away by the collar of his sweat shirt.

"You can't sit there," I told him.

"Why not? The table is empty," he protested.

"No kidding, but the seventh grade team always sits here, and they might be here any minute."

"Do they *own* the restaurant?" Howie asked defiantly.

"Of course not—but they always sit at this table. You don't want to mess with them, Howie. Trust me," I said.

"Well, they aren't going to sit here tonight. Other kids are hungry and thirsty, too. I think it's dumb to make everybody wait around because somebody who *might* show up isn't here yet!" Howie sat down at the table and crossed his arms over his chest.

"Howie, I told you to behave like a normal human," I hissed in his ear.

"I am acting like a human," he whispered back. "One with simple rights."

Why did Al have to make Howie so into moral issues like Mom and Dad? I wondered. With his attitude we'd lose the game for sure!

Howie grabbed me so I'd sit down. I lost

my balance and fell into the chair next to him.

At that moment, Norm Bellini, the captain of the Samurai, and Oscar Novotny, the seventh-grade bully, walked into the ice-cream shop.

"Hey," Oscar said, striding up quickly. "What are you two sitting at our table for?"

"It isn't your table, it's the restaurant's." Howie eyeballed Oscar and Norm.

Norm stared right back at him. "Now look," Norm told Howie. He pointed at a table on the other side of the room that was now empty. "You can sit over there."

"I'm not moving," Howie told him.

"That's what you think!" Oscar countered. "Now get going!"

Oscar raised his fist to sock Howie, but I jumped up in front to defend him. I didn't want Oscar to know how hard Howie's steel-lined jaw was. Oscar socked me right in the mouth. It really didn't hurt that much, though. Oscar isn't half as strong as he thinks he is. But it was still embarrassing to get hit at Frankie's while everybody on both football teams watched.

The manager rushed over to the table. "Hey, Bellini! You and your team aren't welcome here anymore. I saw you hit Timmy. He's younger than you. You're in the seventh

grade, Novotny. You should know better than that.''

Oscar looked at us angrily and mouthed, ''I'm going to get both of you babies on that playing field Sunday!''

''Oh, you think so?'' Howie asked, smirking.

''I know so. The Wolverines are dead meat.'' Oscar sneered at us and all the Samurais walked out together.

FOUR

"You've got to watch who you mouth off to," Al warned Howie the next morning at breakfast.

Howie ignored him and went back to the TV. He was watching an old comedy movie that showed people throwing pies in each other's faces. I hoped he wouldn't try that in the school cafeteria.

My parents, who were preparing to leave for work and had overheard the conversation, were furious with all of us.

"Couldn't you have programmed him to stay out of fights?" my mother asked Al.

"Howie didn't do the fighting. Oscar Novotny did." I attempted to explain the incident in detail.

"Well, I suppose Howie did stand up for

what he morally believed in." My father looked at Howie thoughtfully. "I can see his point."

"Disagreements over things as unimportant as which table one sits at should be settled in a more appropriate manner. The issues at hand were quite petty," my mother muttered.

"They weren't petty to me," Howie informed her.

My mother looked startled, as though she'd never expected Howie to talk back.

Then she and my father kissed all of us quickly and left for work.

"Just stay out of Novotny's way," I told Howie, "and everything will be fine."

"How can I stay out of his way?" Howie asked me. "If he's on the opposing team, I may have to tackle him."

"Except for that!" I snapped. Sometimes I didn't know whether Howie was being smart-mouthed or whether he just didn't know better.

Al left the room for a minute and returned with a Clifton school three-ring notebook, complete with plastic-tabbed manila organizers and a pencil case that attached to the rings. Inside the case were rulers, felt-tip markers, pens, pencils and a sharpener.

"It's time to do some role playing," Al told

Howie. He handed him the notebook. "We're going to act out the first day of school."

Howie did not look enthusiastic. He just sat at the kitchen table and continued to watch television. "You mean I have to go to school every day? Why can't I just stay home and watch TV, like millions of Americans?" he asked.

"You don't have a choice," Al answered. "If you don't go to school, the truant officer will come over here and throw you in reform school. Then my folks will go to jail."

I knew that Al was exaggerating, but we had to convince Howie somehow. "Look," I said, "if you don't go to school, you can't be on the football team. Then you'll never be able to get Oscar." I knew this would hit Howie right where he lived. "C'mon," I told him. "School isn't that terrible. It's fun at recess and lunch. Sometimes we even take field trips."

"Good, tell me what time recess starts, and I'll show up," Howie said.

"You can't only go to recess," I told him.

"Tim's right. If you don't go to your classes, you won't get to play with the Wolverines," Al said.

"Oh, all right. What is this Mrs. Blesinger like?"

"Awful," I answered, remembering how

some kids had pretended to choke themselves last June when they found out they'd be in her class this year. "She's the hardest teacher at school. She loves to pile on homework, give tests and send kids to the principal's office. She's tall and skinny with stringy gray hair. She reminds me of an old witch."

"Don't believe a word of that," Al patted Howie on the shoulder and looked at me with a scowl. "Mrs. Blesinger is a concerned and experienced teacher. She wants each student to live up to his or her potential. Timmy is too lazy to do that—he'd rather fool around."

"That isn't true." I shot Al a dirty look. "I'm just not as smart as the rest of the family. *That's* why I'm not an outstanding student."

"If you put half as much effort into school as you do into learning every baseball player's batting average, I bet you'd be on the honor roll," Al told me.

"I would not. And the honor roll is for creep heads," I insisted.

"It is not," Al squared his shoulders at me. "Jennifer and Neil always make the honor roll," he said in a superior tone.

"They're exceptions to the rule," I said. I'd never quite figured out how those two always managed to shine at both academics and sports. And I'm not that bad of a student. At

Clifton you need at least a C average to get involved in any extracurricular activity. So it's not like I'm flunking.

Howie looked impatient, sitting at the table, leafing through his notebook. "Okay, so how am I supposed to act at school?" he asked.

"Be real polite to Mrs. Blesinger. Always listen and do your homework." Al handed Howie a computerized list of dos and don'ts. "Make Mrs. B. feel like she's wonderful, and don't be afraid to show off your scientific and math knowledge. She likes stuff like that."

"You mean I should recite a list of square roots and chemical elements when we meet?" Howie asked.

"No," Al answered. "Just let your intelligence come out in class. Mrs. Blesinger likes kids that are assertive and to the point. Now, I'll pretend to be Mrs. Blesinger." Al put on one of Mom's scarves and spoke in a falsetto voice. "Good morning, Howie. I see you're new here. Where are you from?"

"I'm from Timmy's basement, California and Japan," Howie said.

"Howie!" I yelled. "Don't tell her that."

"But you said to be to the point. Yesterday you *explicitly* told me I was put together in the basement."

"Leave out the part about the basement,"

I told him. "She'll think you're a weirdo. And you probably shouldn't say anything about Japan. Knowing her, she'll make you give a report on it."

"Well, I sure don't want to get stuck doing extra printouts," Howie said.

"Thanks, Al." I smiled at my brother. "Howie and I have more in common than I thought!"

After a few hours of intense instructions, Howie acted like a typical school kid—except with Howie, you could never be sure how he might wise off.

The next day my father dropped Howie and me off by Clifton's upper-grade entrance. I felt super-excited. In addition to arriving at school with the world's most advanced robot, I wouldn't be considered a little kid anymore. The sixth- through eighth-graders at Clifton have a special wing, their own bathrooms and use a different cafeteria line. It would be nice not to be bumping into a lunch of sticky-fingered kindergartners at lunch every day.

Usually when somebody transfers to Clifton, they go right to the principal's office to take care of all the formalities, but Howie and I went straight to the classroom. Because of the unusual nature of Howie's existence, my folks had already taken care of everything last spring.

Unfortunately, we were a little early, so nobody except Mrs. Blesinger was in the classroom. She looked just as witchy as she had last year. Because Al had been such a hotshot at Clifton, she already knew who I was.

"Hello, Timothy," she said. "Did you have a nice summer?"

"Yes," I answered. Then I whispered to Howie, "Except for the times I thought of her."

"Wow, look at all of these computer stations," Howie said to me. He went over to a desk and opened it.

I followed him. "They're called desks, and you'll be assigned one to sit at," I whispered.

"You mean I can't sit next to you?" Howie looked confused.

"I don't think I've seen you around here before," Mrs. Blesinger said to Howie.

"This is my cousin, Howie Pentergasser," I told her. "He's living with us this year. His parents are traveling around the world, studying ozone or something like that," I explained.

At that moment, Mrs. B looked like she had just won a million dollars. "I'm so honored to have two young men from the Watkins gene pool in my classroom!" Mrs. Blesinger shook both of our hands. "I'm expecting big things from both of you."

I felt like throwing up, but Howie seemed totally taken in by her interest. I could tell by the sickeningly happy look on his face.

"I've heard wonderful things about you," Howie told her. "Albert thinks you're the best teacher he's ever had."

"My opinion about him is likewise. He'll *always* be my best student," Mrs. Blesinger crooned. "I still remember the solar generator that won a blue ribbon in the Midwest Science Fair. . . ." Mrs. Blesinger turned toward me. "Tell me, has Al built anything that exceptional since?"

"No," I answered. "He's been very involved with computers lately." If she only knew she was talking to another one of Albert's creations!

"Do you love science and mathematics, too?" Mrs. Blesinger asked both of us.

"I'm astounded by all the dynamics of the universe," Howie said. Then he handed her a folder of phony school records that Al and my mother had printed for him.

I didn't say anything. I figured she'd find out about the difference in my skills and Al's soon enough.

After looking through Howie's records, Mrs. Blesinger had that million-dollar look on her face again. "These scores are incredible! I've never seen anything like them in my whole career—not even Al's scores were this good. I suppose you'll want to be in Future Scientists of America—they meet Wednesday after school. And then there's the Junior Physics League on Tuesday night."

"I don't think so," Howie told her. "I'm tied up with the Wolverines, and I think I'll try out for the track team. Mr. Rumbaugh mentioned something about baseball in the spring."

Mrs. B looked at Howie with horror. "How could you let your precious brain cells waste away like that?"

I tried hard not to burst out laughing and looked out the window. If only Mrs. Blesinger knew that Howie was only a piece of electronic machinery! She'd die if she knew that Albert had concocted the file, including the test scores—with my mother's help, no less.

Soon the first bell rang and the other kids started streaming into the room. Everybody sat down where they wanted, but Mrs. Blesinger quickly reassigned seats to each of us alphabetically.

Since my name is near the end of the alphabet, I got seated in the back by the window, which was a row away from Howie. I love sitting there. It means I can goof off without the teacher noticing. Howie was placed right smack between Melinda Peavy and Sharon Rawson.

I overheard Sharon say something about "terrific" and "football" to Howie. He smiled at her and at Melinda. Then he bleeped.

The whole class laughed and looked around the room. Nobody could tell that he'd made the noise, and Howie acted as if nothing had happened. He looked around the room, too.

Mrs. Blesinger stomped up to the front of the room. "Who's doing that? You all know that radios are not allowed at school."

Everybody remained silent. I almost choked from trying to stifle a laugh. And Howie bleeped again.

"Whoever is doing this will be in big trouble." Mrs. Blesinger was on the warpath now. "One more noise from that radio and we'll *all* stay after. This is *not* the way to start the first day of school."

I shot Howie the meanest look I could think of, and quickly flashed the remote-control box at him. He grinned at me until he saw I was serious. Then he turned back around and smiled at Mrs. Blesinger. Howie would certainly liven up sixth grade.

When Mrs. Blesinger calmed down, she started lecturing us on the privileges of being an upper-school student. The only part that sounded halfway interesting was that we'd now be allowed to go to dances and take part in school government.

"Now," she said, "every day in my class we look up a word in the dictionary. You should have one in your desk. Today's word is *infinite*." She wrote it on the blackboard, her chalk squeaking. A few kids groaned as they opened their desks.

Immediately, without opening his desk, Howie raised his hand.

"Yes, Howard," Mrs. Blesinger looked startled. "Do you have a question?"

"*Infinite* means endless and extending indefinitely," he said.

"Good," she answered and went on to explain examples of *infinite*. "Suppose we wanted to count all of the grains of sand in the box in the play yard. That would be an infinite number."

"No," Howie interrupted.

"I beg your pardon?" Now Mrs. Blesinger looked perturbed.

"If you counted long enough, you'd reach the number of grains of sand eventually," Howie pointed out.

"Yeah," Sharon agreed. "If we emptied the box and each took a big jarful and counted for years, we'd probably reach the final number."

51

"Let's go outside and start counting!" Howie suggested.

"Great idea," someone else agreed, and a bunch of the kids stood up.

"Everybody sit down!" Mrs. Blesinger ordered. Then she gave a new example for *infinite*—the amount of detentions we'd all receive if we didn't behave.

Thank goodness Howie didn't correct her on that.

We spent the rest of the morning getting our textbooks and listening to Mrs. Blesinger tell us what an exciting challenge sixth grade would be. Around eleven-thirty she gave us our first assignment.

"People," she said. "So I can know best how to help you with your arithmetic skills this year, I'll be giving you a test to see how well you know your multiplication facts. This test, of course, won't count as a grade. It's for me to see what you've forgotten over the summer."

Howie made a silly face at me, and I held my hand to my stomach as though I were going to be sick. I couldn't believe that at eleven-thirty in the morning, the first day of school, I was being tested on multiplication facts. I practically fell off of my chair at 11:32, when Howie handed in the test.

Howie's speed in finishing the assignment

gave Mrs. B a new reason to lecture us. "I hope everybody in this class takes the time to check his or her paper. Now that you're in the sixth grade, I shouldn't have to even remind you of that."

"But I did check it over," Howie argued.

"Nobody can do fifty multiplication problems correctly in two minutes," Mrs. Blesinger told Howie.

"I can," Howie answered impatiently.

Mrs. B stared at Howie for a minute, then began pacing in front of the room. "Class, sometimes we may do our math quickly because we want to get it over with, but I wouldn't if I were you. Because each of you will have to correct each problem you get wrong, and then write it over again four times," she told us.

Everybody groaned and went back to work quickly. I swear I'm allergic to multiplication. I kept erasing and changing my answers. I accidentally made a hole under eight times nine, I'd changed it so much. I considered crumpling the paper in my pocket and having Howie do it at lunchtime, but I didn't.

Howie went back to his seat for about thirty seconds before handing the paper in again. Mrs. Blesinger looked at Howie with exasperation, but I knew he had gotten a one-hundred. His processor knew the answer to any math problem.

My mind, on the other hand, had gone into low gear over the summer. Then I realized it didn't matter how many I missed. I could have Howie correct my work that night!

FIVE

When the bell rang for lunch, everybody rushed toward the door. It was as though none of us had eaten since last week. I was starving. I'd only had a sip of papaya juice and a granola muffin before leaving for school.

"Nobody leaves until I have twenty-six papers on my desk," Mrs. Blesinger commanded. The way she counted them, you'd have thought each one was a hundred-dollar bill. "I'll hand these back after lunch. You are dismissed."

I was glad I'd decided against walking out of the room with the test. I could have been in big trouble. Obviously Mrs. Blesinger's many years of teaching had made her aware of most kids' tricks.

Howie escaped from the room a few seconds before I did and waited by my locker.

I took out our money for lunch. "Wow, you really had Mrs. Blesinger going," I told Howie. "It should only take you a sec to do my corrections tonight."

"You want me to *what*?" Howie asked.

I repeated myself, hoping Howie would hear me this time. The hallway was noisy with kids slamming lockers and rushing down the hall.

"What makes you think I'm doing your math homework for you?" Howie asked.

"Because it's easy for you. That's why," I said.

"So?" Howie answered. "That doesn't mean I'm a walking, talking pocket calculator that lives for your convenience."

"You mean you aren't going to do it?"

"You got it." Howie waved at some of the guys on the team who were already on the flight of stairs ahead of us. "Save us a seat!" he shouted.

"Some friend you are. Your processor does math in seconds and you won't even help me," I said.

"You have a processor, too." Howie pointed to my head. "You should learn to use it."

I wanted to clobber Howie, but the floors at Clifton are hard tile and I couldn't risk him going out of control there like he had at home when he fell.

"You are totally ungrateful," I told him. "You're sleeping in my room, wearing my clothes, plus I got you the best position on the Wolverines. You could at least do me a little favor."

"I won't be doing you any favor if I correct those problems." Howie said. He was acting just like Al. Whenever Al helps me with math, he stands over my shoulder and makes *me* do all the work. He claims it's good for me.

"And," Howie added, "I could have gotten the quarterback position on the Wolverines without your help."

Howie was acting too much like a regular person now. I wished Al hadn't designed him to be such an individual. As soon as we got to the first floor, we both raced toward the cafeteria line.

"Hey!" a teacher called out to us. "Walk! There's enough food for everybody."

The line was already outside the cafeteria into the hallway. Some kids stood against the wall quietly, but most kids pushed and shoved and shouted.

"Quiet!" said the same teacher who had told us to slow down. "There are classes going on across the hall."

I was so mad at Howie that I didn't even

want to stand in line with him, but he took the place in front of me. Then, without warning, he rushed out of the line, darted through the doorway and pushed himself in front of the steam table, which was near the center of the line. I followed him, but it was too late to stop him.

"I want a BLT on whole wheat . . . and hold the mayo," Howie yelled to Lulu, the head lunchroom cook.

"Get back in line—I'm in no mood for practical jokes today," Lulu told him. "I'm short-handed. And, Timothy Watkins," she said, glaring at me, "you know better than to allow your friends to pull shenanigans like that."

Everybody was looking at us and laughing. I wished the tiles on the floor would open up and swallow me.

"You can't do that," I informed Howie as I tugged him back to the end of the line. The line was longer now, and we were much farther back.

"Why was she so bent out of shape?" Howie asked.

"This isn't a restaurant," I said. "You can only order what's on the menu board. And whatever you do, don't cut in line!"

For the next few seconds Howie stood next to me quietly. I kept my eye on him and listened to some eighth-grade girls behind me

58

discuss the guys in their classes. It sounded like the guys were either awesome and breathtaking or else hopelessly ugly nerds.

Mrs. Riley, the assistant principal, walked by us and waved to me. I guess I'm kind of a celebrity because of Al.

Then Howie raced out of line again toward the steam table. Mrs. Riley had cut the line and was just getting her silverware.

I quickly followed him.

Howie tapped Mrs. Riley on the shoulder. "Hey, you have to wait your turn," he told her. "Get back in line," he said, gesturing toward the hallway.

I ran up just as Mrs. Riley spoke. "Young man, what is your name?" she asked.

"Howie Pentergasser," he answered.

"Uh, he's my cousin," I hurried to explain. "He just moved here, and he's never been in a cafeteria like this before today."

"Well, Timmy, if it were anybody else he'd get a detention. But I know you aren't a troublemaker." She smiled. "Have a productive year."

I yanked Howie back to the end of the line again. "What do you think you were doing? You don't tell the assistant principal what to do!" I said, irritated.

"But she was pushing in front of everybody," Howie complained.

"She can stand wherever she wants to. And so can teachers. Didn't Al program you to tell the difference between them and kids?"

"Of course he did," Howie answered. "But I don't think it's fair for them to get in front of us."

"I don't, either," I agreed, "but there isn't much we can do about it."

Howie grinned. "Let's start a protest march for equal rights for kids!" he suggested.

"Let's not. And if you don't behave," I whispered in his ear, "I'm turning you off."

The line moved along slowly and my stomach grumbled. I looked up at the cafeteria, not sure if I should have the baked spaghetti or a hamburger.

Lunch at Clifton costs fifty-five cents; it includes an entree, salad, milk and dessert. My friends think school food is reheated garbage, but both Al and I look forward to school lunches since Mom only cooks vegetarian food. We're allowed to eat whatever we want away from home, as long as we don't bring it into the house. Lunch is my favorite time at school, and Howie was doing a good job of ruining it.

I took a hamburger, some french fries, a container of cole slaw, an orange cupcake and milk.

Howie took the hamburger lunch, a spaghetti plate, a brownie and three containers of milk. I was so mad at him, I didn't care how much he stuffed into his trash compactor. I didn't care if it broke.

Then Howie pranced out of the line without paying.

"Catch that kid!" the cashier yelled.

Mrs. Riley went after Howie and brought him back over to me. "Timothy, I hope you'll teach your cousin some of the rules at Clifton. We pay for our lunch before we eat."

I had to think fast. "I'm sorry, Mrs. Riley. You see, Howie lived on a commune and he doesn't understand certain things." I figured she'd believe this, knowing my folks.

Mrs. Riley was instantly sympathetic. She put her hand on Howie's shoulder. "Dear, things are very different in normal society. Timmy will teach you how things are."

The cashier wasn't so nice about it. I had to pay for three lunches—both of Howie's and mine.

I surveyed the cafeteria as we entered the lunchroom. The Wolverines were seated at two big tables, and the cheerleaders were at a table across from them. Susi and Jennifer usually join us at the players' table, but I didn't see them around.

I placed my tray next to Josh, and Howie sat at the same table, but at the other end. I'm glad we weren't sitting next to each other. I didn't want to talk to him, or have the other guys know why I was sore at him.

The Samurai team had already finished lunch. They walked past our table without saying a word.

"Looks like they forgot all about yesterday," Josh said. He stuffed a cupcake into his mouth.

"I doubt it," I answered. "Oscar Novotny's brain might be the size of a sesame seed, but he wouldn't forget getting thrown out of Frankie's." I thought he'd probably beat Howie up sometime that week or wallop him in the game. At this point it didn't matter. I was so mad at Howie I wished that I could switch him off forever, put him in the basement and bring him back as something for show and tell.

But it seemed like everyone else wanted to give Howie plenty of attention.

"You should have seen the look on the witch's face when you handed in that test!" Neil grimaced at Howie and imitated Mrs. Blesinger in a cackly voice. "Class . . ."

"Hey, Howie, did you order worms today?" Noah asked.

Howie picked up a strand of spaghetti and waved it in the air. "They're delish when you have them with melted cheese and blood!" he said.

Everybody started laughing. *That's an old*

joke, I told myself. Al could have programmed Howie to be more original—in addition to a few other things.

For the next few minutes kids tried to top each other with yucky food stories.

As soon as we were finished, a group of short, thin-looking football players jumped onto an empty table across from us. I couldn't tell for sure if they were male or female through the wire on the masks of their football helmets. But when long reddish hair fell out of one of the players' helmets and onto her shoulders I knew it was the Samurais' cheerleaders for sure.

"One, two, three, four, who aren't we for? Five, six, seven, eight, who will we obliterate? Wolverines! Wolverines! Wolverines!"

The girls stuck their tongues out and turned cartwheels across the cafeteria floor. Then, in high falsetto voices, they sang, "They can't even block our path. Sixth-grade boys use bubble bath!"

Quickly they raced out the lunchroom door. We all chased them toward the cafeteria doorway, but we were blocked by Lulu.

A mean smile lit up Lulu's face. "Did you boys forget to take your trays back? The cafeteria rules haven't changed since last year, you know."

We crept back to the table and cleaned it up.

"Don't worry," Howie said. "We'll knock the wind out of their sails."

"You better believe it," I agreed.

"What do you have planned?" Josh asked.

"Oh, Tim and I will think of something," Howie assured everyone.

I felt less angry with Howie after that.

When we got back to the room, our math tests were on our desks, facedown. I could tell by the red marks showing through that I'd missed plenty. I craned my neck to see Howie's paper. He had a big yellow smily face and a gold star on his.

"Wow!" Sharon squealed. "It's like you're a mixture of Timmy and his brilliant brother."

"You're awesome," Melinda agreed, smiling at Howie and batting her eyelashes.

Maybe I wasn't a genius. But at least I didn't have to put up with Melinda Peavy drooling all over me!

SIX

"Let's see your math paper," Howie said when we got home.

"I thought you weren't going to do it for me." I opened the refrigerator and poured some homemade carob syrup into two glasses of milk.

"I won't do it myself, but I'll be glad to help you." He looked over my paper. "You seem to have the most problems with the nines table."

"It's the hardest." I pushed a glass of carob milk over to Howie and took a sip of my own.

"Actually the nines are the easiest," Howie told me. "They're like doing a magic trick."

"Maybe to you they are. You were built with a calculator in your head!" I reminded him.

"Now watch me." Howie wrote down two times nine. "What's the answer to that?"

"Eighteen," I told him. "I'm not *that* bad at arithmetic."

"Then what's nine times seven?"

"I always get that one mixed up," I said. "I think it's fifty-seven."

Howie wrote that down, too. "Nine times seven is sixty-three," he said.

He pointed to the answer. "Do you notice anything similar about eighteen and sixty-three? Just look at them carefully."

After I studied the numbers for a minute, I saw that the numerals six and three added up to nine, and so did one plus eight.

"On these two problems the numerals in the product add up to nine," I told him. "So what?"

"They should on all facts where nine is the multiplier or multiplicand, or your answer is incorrect." Howie wrote down all the nine facts and their answers. "Now see if you can find another pattern," Howie said.

1	2	3	4	5	6	7	8	9
×9	×9	×9	×9	×9	×9	×9	×9	×9
9	18	27	36	45	54	63	72	81

I looked over the problems carefully, noticing that the numeral in the tens column was

67

always one less than the one in the multiplicand. "Wow, there is a pattern here," I said.

"Just remind yourself that the number in the tens column should be one less than the multiplier. Whatever other number added to it that makes nine should be the numeral in the ones column," Howie told me, pointing to the products.

"That's a good trick," I said.

Howie turned over the paper. "What's nine times nine?" he asked.

I thought it over for a moment. "It's eighty-one."

"Five times nine?"

"Forty-five?"

"Good. You seem to be getting it. Unfortunately, nine is the only number you can do that with, so I'll go over your other mistakes with you."

"Thanks, Howie."

"Don't thank me. Have a better attitude toward arithmetic. It's fun. It's only a matter of figuring things out and then practicing them—like in football," he said.

Howie drew up some diagrams of football plays while I corrected my homework. Howie might be right about applying the same amount of work to math and football, but I still thought football was more fun.

On the way to practice, Howie and I

68

stopped off at Nichols Sporting Goods to pick up his uniform. I had given him an extra pair of cleats that still fit me, so we didn't need to buy Howie a pair. Howie looked like a pro in his red-and-white uniform.

He proudly carried the play diagrams on large sheets of paper which he had rolled up. I felt almost like a high-school player. Nobody else on the team had ever brought in play descriptions written on paper. I couldn't wait to see what the other kids would say.

"Hey, here's Mr. Superkid," Neil greeted Howie. "I never met anybody who could play ball, stand up to Oscar Novotny *and* ace math tests."

"We had a lot of math drills where I came from," Howie answered. "And I brushed up in summer school."

"Yech." Neil made a face. "You mean you had to serve an extended prison term!"

Howie shrugged. "My parents made me go."

"I bet they didn't offer a brush-up course in punching out jerks like Oscar Novotny," Josh said. "I bet there's nobody else like him in the whole United States."

"I don't know," Howie answered. "Whenever there are kids, there are bullies. It's a fact of life."

We all turned to watch the cheerleaders as

they pranced onto the field. Today they had dressed in their uniforms, consisting of white sweaters with wolverine paw-print appliqués and red-and-white pleated skirts.

Sharon Rawson walked right up to us. "Hi, Howie. You look great in your uniform."

All the other girls stood around Howie to admire him. And Howie sure knew how to turn the charm on girls—although Al certainly couldn't have taught him that. He thanked them for the cheer they did for him yesterday and told them he'd never seen such incredible cheerleaders before, which was the absolute truth. He'd never seen *any* cheerleaders before yesterday's practice.

"And you've got the most gorgeous blue eyes any of us has ever seen," Sharon told him.

I glanced at Howie. Al had made Howie's eyes so blue that they looked almost fake to me.

Coach Rumbaugh blew his whistle. "All Wolverines over here! We've got lots of work to do on strategy today. The game's this Sunday. Anybody have any ideas?"

"I do!" Howie raised his hand.

"Good," the coach answered. "Tell us about it."

Howie stood up in front of the team members and unrolled his diagram. Everyone listened closely. It was amazing how quickly Howie had gained the respect of everybody. Susi busily took notes.

"The Samurai probably think we're a bunch of goats—especially now that we're without that Crusher kid. And because we're younger, the Samurai think they're better," Howie said. "But most of what the Samurai have is an overinflated opinion of their abilities. I caught a glimpse of them playing yesterday. They aren't such great shakes."

"Yeah!" Noah shouted. "We'll demolish them."

"I bet they're a bunch of clumsy idiots," Josh agreed.

"Don't underestimate them," Susi warned us.

"Susi's right," Howie told everybody. "That's why we have to make sure we have a plan. Since we haven't played them yet this year, we don't know what to expect from them. They'll probably do some standard formations, but I think we can do better than that."

The kids all listened intently to Howie, as though whatever he said would work. On one hand, I felt proud that I'd brought Howie to Clifton, but on the other hand, I felt jealous of him. At this moment, Howie the android was receiving more respect than I'd been

71

given as captain of the team. For a moment I wanted to say, "Who *is* captain here?"

Howie unrolled one of the tubes of paper he'd been carrying with him. "The first play is called the 'all-around deceptive draw.' Fooling the Samurai is ninety-eight point three percent of winning, and this play will trick them for sure. Once I give somebody the ball, they'll pretend to pass it to somebody else, but end up handing it back to me."

"Big deal," Noah said. "they'll just sack you or the kid with the ball."

"No, they won't," Howie told him. The original person with the ball will pull the ball down and hand it to me. I'll tuck it away and run with it. The Samurai will have been so intent on sacking the original holder, they won't know what's coming off. By the time they realize they've been drawn in, I'll be long gone. We'll call this play 'DD Ninety-Eight Point Three'."

"What if they sack you, anyway?" Noah asked.

"They won't," answered Howie. "Nobody on their team runs as fast as I do."

"I'll buy that," Susi said with a hint of sarcasm in her voice. "No kid does."

Howie and I looked at each other in surprise. We were the only two kids who knew the truth—that Howie had been wired to run

72

like a top high-school kid. I felt uneasy about what Susi had just said.

"Sounds good," Coach Rumbaugh said, nodding his head. "Pentergasser, Barclay, Garland, Watkins. I want to see you guys try it." He blew his whistle. "First team, you've got the ball. Second team on defense."

Howie's play was dynamite. Even though you knew what was going to happen, it was hard not to be taken by surprise. And Howie could really run with that ball. We also tried the play with Jennifer, and she easily scored a touchdown.

During our break, Susi called me over. Howie stayed on the field and practiced running with the ball.

Susi pulled me close as if she wanted to ask me something private. "Is your cousin on steroids?" she asked.

"What?" I couldn't believe I'd heard her right.

"On steroids. You know, those drugs that make people run faster and lift more weights and stuff."

"Of course not," I answered. "Why would you think that? Howie's just in terrific shape. He works out a lot at home." I did not like the way Susi sounded at all.

Susi pulled out something she had copied from a football book. "I checked a rate chart for running speed and passing. Only superior seventeen- and eighteen-year-olds can throw a ball eighty yards and run the fifty in five and a half seconds flat. Maybe your cousin is really older than us and only looks young."

"Why would you say that?" I asked.

"He aced that test Mrs. Blesinger gave us— in two minutes. I bet he's not really your cousin," she said.

I gulped. Al had over-programmed him. I'd have to remember to tell Al to do another rewiring to downgrade Howie's abilities. "Then who do you think Howie is?" I asked.

"Maybe he's some kind of spy," Susi told me. "I saw this detective show where there had been drug dealing at a school, and they planted a young-looking cop there to work undercover."

"Susi, I think you watch too much television. Howie is my cousin, and a bona fide sixth-grader. If you don't believe it, I'll show you his records and a copy of his birth certificate," I declared.

"Well, maybe he is for real. But whoever he is, I think what you did to Jennifer was cruddy. She should have been quarterback. She's been on the team since third grade!" Susi argued.

"No offense, Susi, but I don't think we'd

beat the Samurais with a girl as our quarter-back.''

Susi rolled her eyes. ''You are a male chauvinist hog, Timothy Watkins, and so is your cousin. So there!''

''I am not!'' I said angrily.

''You are so!''

''Am not. Besides, the coach is impressed with Howie,'' I reminded her. ''Very impressed.''

Susi made a face and an oinking sound at me.

''And,'' I said, ''you could have cared less about Jennifer until she told you she wanted to be quarterback. You sure didn't think of her for the job right away, like when you called me a few days ago. You were panicking!''

''My mind was boggled,'' Susi protested. ''Losing Crusher and all. I have a lot of responsibilities that make it easier for you to play ball. If it wasn't for me, you couldn't keep your equipment straight.''

The two of us kept bickering until Coach Rumbaugh noticed. He hates arguments between team members because it's bad for team spirit. ''What's going on over here?'' he asked.

''Oh, we're just discussing a school assignment,'' I said.

"Good," Coach answered. "I like to see our key members thinking about grades on the first day of the school term. You going to make sure you keep them up, Timmy?"

"I promise. No trouble this year," I said. I hoped that would be true.

Coach Rumbaugh is also in charge of baseball and soccer. You're not allowed to participate in anything extracurricular at Clifton if you're having trouble with academics. When I was trying to learn long division the spring before, I had missed some important baseball practices.

"Does anybody have any more useful strategies we can work on today?" the coach asked when break ended and we were all seated on the bench.

"I've got two more," Howie announced.

All eyes were on Howie again as he rolled out the diagrams. "This first one is called the 'phony, far-out lateral pass.' We pretend to throw the ball to one player, then to another player, until it actually reaches a third player. That player runs it to the goal. Nobody is going to expect that on a lateral. Jennifer should be the last runner on this play, because she's got the second fastest legs, and I want to pass it to her. We'll call it 'PFB-Three'."

A half-smile crossed Jennifer's face.

The next play Howie described was called the "rattrap sneak." We'd permit their defensive tackle to crash through us, then come after him immediately and bring him down. Howie explained the tactic would work best if we could do it to Novotny. By knocking him over, we'd bring the Samurai to the ground.

"Let's try the rattrap first and practice our tackling," Coach ordered. "And don't be afraid to knock people over. Remember . . . the team that hits the hardest wins."

We divided up into offense and defense and took our positions. The coach blew the whistle.

Jennifer snapped the ball to Howie, who took it and broke through the line. Helmets clacked as we tackled Howie. Six of us piled on top of him. Howie squirmed to get out from underneath.

"Get off me, you guys!" he hollered.

Coach Rumbaugh rushed over to Howie. "What's wrong?" he asked.

"My arm, it's killing me," Howie said.

"Can you move it?" The coach looked concerned.

Howie wiggled his fingers, but his arm wasn't moving.

"Are you serious?" I asked. "You can't move it?"

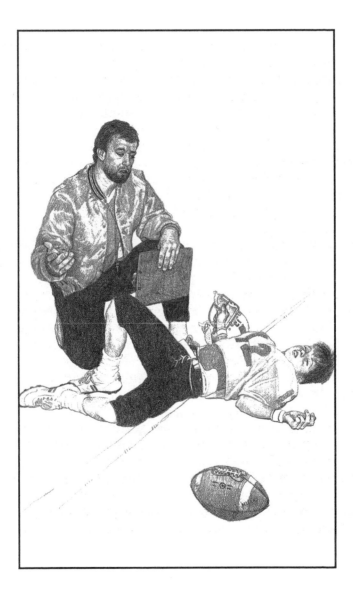

"Ow, it hurts!" Howie whined. It looked like he was hurting for real. He had that strained look on his face, the one guys get when they're in pain and trying hard not to cry.

"Let me talk to him alone for a second," I said.

Everybody walked away. I could see them whispering to each other. I knew some of the kids were probably enjoying the incident. Not that anyone would want someone to get hurt, but I know stuff like that is kind of thrilling. I find other kids' accidents exciting myself.

"Are you faking this or what?" I asked.

"Something snapped in my arm. And I feel a little dizzy. My motor must have been thrown off. Just get me out of here—fast!"

The coach tapped me on the shoulder. "I'll drive you and Howie over to Northside Hospital. It's not far."

"No," Howie answered sharply.

"It doesn't look like you can wait on this. And I'm responsible if anything happens to you," Coach Rumbaugh said.

"We better go home," I said. "Howie's family doesn't like him going to strange hospitals."

"Timothy, I know kids don't like hospitals, but we can't play around with this." The coach sounded angry now. "We're dealing with a serious injury here."

"I'll be okay," Howie assured him. "It feels better already."

"I guarantee you'll be okay, because I'm taking you over to Northside. Everybody else go home now. Practice is over!" Coach Rumbaugh roared.

The kids drifted away slowly so that they could watch what was going on.

"Get going!" the coach shouted to them. Then he ushered us across the field and toward the parking lot. "My car is the big blue one with the Bears sticker on the fender."

I had to think quickly again. My folks weren't home yet, and my only hope was Al.

"Uh, I better see if my dad's home. He'd want to be at the hospital," I told Coach Rumbaugh.

"I'm sure Uncle Peter would want that." Howie's speech sounded slightly slurred.

Potowatamie's fieldhouse has a phone near the doorway. The coach gave me a quarter, and I called Al. I thanked my lucky stars that the coach didn't stand next to me so that he could hear. He seemed more concerned with Howie. And I was glad that Al was at home.

"Uh . . . hi, Dad," I said. "Something happened to Howie."

Al caught on right away. "What's wrong, Tim?" he asked.

"Howie got hurt on the field. He broke his arm and may have gotten a concussion," I said.

Al made his voice sound more adult. "Please have Mr. Rumbaugh discuss the matter with me. Is he available?"

I motioned for the coach to come to the phone, and I stayed with Howie.

"What are they gonna do, Timmy? My processor is acting haywire."

"Don't worry, and be quiet," I said.

A few seconds later, Coach Rumbaugh told us how the situation would be handled. "We're supposed to take you right home, and your dad will take you to the hospital. I feel better now that I talked to him."

On the way home, Howie sat in the back and said nothing. I kept thinking about what a close call this one was. When we got there, my dad's van was in front of the house with the keys in the ignition. *Weird*, I told myself. My folks almost always take public transportation to save energy and money, and leave the van in the garage. It was way too early for either one of them to be home. Even if Al had beeped one of them somehow, they could not have arrived home this fast.

Al ran out of the house the minute he saw the coach's car drive up.

"Dad will be out in a second," he told us. "And he thanks you for your concern, Coach."

"Good luck, Howie." Coach put his hand on Howie's shoulder. "Sorry you won't be able to play Sunday." He shook Al's hand. "Nice meeting you."

"Who says he won't play?" Al said under his breath and opened the back of the van. He lifted Howie in as the coach drove away.

"What the heck is going on here?" I asked Al.

"I drove Dad's van out here so that your coach would think we were going to drive Howie to the emergency room."

"You don't have a license," I told him.

"So?" Al answered. "Nobody else was home and I had to make this look convincing. It worked, didn't it?"

"Shut up, you guys. I'm falling apart," Howie complained.

Al's caper with the van surprised me. I hadn't realized how sly he could be. Maybe he wasn't such a nerd, after all.

SEVEN

Fortunately, the only injuries to Howie were a snapped-out bolt in his right arm and a few loose wires. Al fixed them immediately.

"How are we supposed to explain this to everybody?" I asked Al.

"Just tell the kids he has a slightly strained ligament. Today is Wednesday. That should heal by the end of the week." Al wrapped a bandage around Howie's arm.

"Can you remember that, Howie?" I asked.

Howie grinned.

"And, Howie, you've got to avoid being tackled," Al told him.

"Doesn't everyone try to avoid getting tackled in football?" Howie asked.

"But you've got to be really careful. You

can't get into situations that could land you in the hospital," Al explained. "That's one of the reasons I've rigged you to run so fast."

"About his running and general performance level . . . I think you ought to reprogram him into the normal range," I said.

Howie looked indignant. "Absolutely not. I like being the best."

I knew exactly how he felt about that. It had taken me a long time to gain enough respect from the kids to be made team captain, and I wasn't thrilled about sharing the spotlight with Howie. Of course, I knew it was my mistake for suggesting he be quarterback. Then I felt a little foolish about being jealous of Howie. He wasn't even a real kid!

Al didn't want to downgrade Howie, either. "By making Howie excel at everything, we'll give the other kids something to strive for. In addition to Mom's desire that Howie be an answer to world serenity, Howie could be the ideal of every kid," he said.

I thought about Howie's antics that day at lunch in the cafeteria. The way he'd been behaving and bleeping earlier would not make him anybody's idol. If Al's model child had another day like today, he'd end up in permanent detention. The more I thought about the incident in the cafeteria, the more I thought I should start bringing bag lunches.

Then I remembered the seventh-grade cheerleaders' performance earlier, and I wondered if Howie was really creative enough to dream up something juicy to do to them.

"Hey, Howie. How are we going to get revenge on the Samurais?" I asked.

"I believe a repeat of their data in a high-grade form would teach them an embarrassing lesson," Howie said.

"Speak English, not computerese."

"I was thinking of mocking them by throwing a motorized football at them—that they can't catch. It could fly across the entire cafeteria. We could have our cheerleaders throw it, and have Al clone some more girls," Howie suggested.

"Are you totally out of your main processor?" Al asked. "Do you know how long it takes to make one android? Even the motorized football would take a few days."

"Come on, Al," Howie chided. "Don't be a party pooper."

"Just the motorized football. Please, Al?" I asked.

"You two are crazy," Al told us, and went upstairs to work on his calculus homework.

I thought over Howie's idea. It was good, but impractical. I'd love to see Oscar Novotny chasing a wild football around the cafeteria. Then a brain wave flashed through my mind.

"Howie, have you ever heard of a slime football?" I asked.

"A what?"

"Remember that movie you were watching, where they threw pies at each other? This football will be similar. We can fill it with cottage cheese, bean gunk and mustard. And when we throw it at Oscar, the whole thing will splat in his face."

"Sort of like a football meltdown. We'll reverse what they did and dress up like cheerleaders when we do it. That'll make them look really wimpy. What's Sharon Rawson's access code?" Howie picked up the phone. "We could call her about the uniforms now."

I liked Howie's idea, but he was too enthusiastic about calling Sharon.

"*I'll* call her," I informed Howie and looked through the phone book on the kitchen shelf. I found her number under Joseph Rawson on Edgewood, and dialed. Then this strange feeling zigzagged through my body before the phone started ringing, and I hung up. Except for Susi Weiland, I'd never phoned a girl my age before.

"Is her modem busy?" Howie grabbed the phone. "Maybe I'll have better luck."

"Uh, I think we should wait a few minutes." Then I rushed into the bathroom and practiced a speech to Sharon in front of the mirror.

"Hi, this is Tim Watkins. Remember me? Howie and I wanted to get even with the seventh-grade cheerleaders, and I thought I'd ask you a favor."

No good, I told myself. I slicked my hair back with a damp comb and squared my shoulders. Now, I felt more confident. "Hi, Sharon, this is Tim. Since you're the head cheerleader, and I'm the football captain, I'm wondering if . . ."

Howie pounded a fist on the bathroom door. "What's going on in here? Are we going to see if Sharon's modem is clear or not?"

"Hold your horses. And it's called a phone, Howie." I checked myself again in the mirror and unlocked the bathroom door.

"I don't see why you won't let me try," Howie complained. "I want a chance to use the phone."

"When I'm done calling Sharon, you can give Josh or Noah a call."

Howie emitted an annoyed bleep while I redialed Sharon. Her mother answered the phone on the third ring.

"Hello?"

"Uh, this is Timothy Watkins. I'd like to talk with Sharon," I mumbled.

"Sharon isn't home right now," her mother

told me. "Would you like to leave a message?"

"Tell her Tim called about football." I left my number and hung up. So much for my first attempt at calling a girl.

Later at dinner, we had a slight problem with Howie.

"I'm not pleased with the fact that you've programmed Howie to eat at every meal," my mother informed Albert.

"Why not?" both Al and I asked.

"Because it's a waste of food. Howie runs on batteries, not calories," my father reminded us.

"Then what am I supposed to do with him at lunchtime?" I asked.

"Yeah, the kids will think I'm a weirdo if I tell them I'm on a starvation diet," Howie said.

My parents pondered the problem during our dinner of tofu, vegetables and rice. Al came up with a perfect solution while my mother was serving slices of thickly frosted carrot cake.

"Howie could be reprogrammed to eat only in social situations," Al told us. "And when he's with the family he can sit and watch."

"Great idea," I answered, grabbing Howie's piece of cake.

"I'm still programmed to eat," Howie complained.

"And one piece of cake is enough," my mother said, frowning at me.

The phone rang and Al ran to answer it. He came back to the table, smirking. "Woo, woo, woo! Telephone for Timmy, and it's a girl."

The entire family looked at me. I was so nervous about talking to Sharon, I couldn't move.

"If you don't want to talk to her, I will," Howie volunteered.

"I'm capable of carrying on a telephone conversation," I said, standing up. I pulled the phone into the family room and shut the door.

"I'm so glad that you called," Sharon told me, "because I was thinking about you, Tim."

"Really?" I asked.

"Um hum—and Howie, too. How is he?"

"He's fine. He just got a strained ligament. He'll be able to play on Sunday," I told her.

"I'm so glad. The reason I was thinking of both of you is that I'm having a party Saturday night," Sharon said.

"I thought your birthday was in the spring," I said.

"This isn't a birthday party. It's a football party. I thought we should celebrate the big game. I hope you and your cousin can come. I especially want Howie to be there, since he's new in town."

"Hold on a sec." I walked back into the dining room and put my hand over the receiver. "Sharon Rawson is having a party Saturday. Can I go?"

"Of course, Timmy, but only if Howard is invited. It wouldn't be nice to leave him alone," my mother said.

"Believe me, he's invited. You don't need to worry about Howie's social life."

"Wow, my first chance to completely interface!" Howie sounded excited. "I didn't think I'd experience that mode so soon."

I walked back into the family room to continue the conversation privately. "We'll be there," I told her.

"Good. It's at five o'clock, for dinner. What was your call about?"

"Remember what those Samurai cheerleaders did to us today at lunchtime?"

"That was so annoying," Sharon said.

"Howie and I thought up a way to get them back. We need your uniforms." I explained the plan in detail.

"You and your cousin are so original!" Sharon giggled. "Consider it done." Then she hung up.

I flashed an "okay" sign to Howie when I returned to the table and he smiled.

After I finished my carrot cake, my mother looked at me. "There's something I'd like to rap about with you in private after we clean up," she said.

A little later she ushered me upstairs to my room. My parents have this agreement with us about not discussing important matters until after dinner. I did not like the look on Mom's face. It reminded me of the time I got a D in arithmetic. I wondered if she'd found out that I'd done poorly on my first math test.

My mother studied my face for a moment as though I'd disappointed her somehow. "Timothy, today I ran into Mrs. Ellison at the food co-op."

"How's she doing?" I asked. I had an idea of where the conversation would lead.

"She's fine, but Jennifer is quite upset about something. I think you may be somewhat responsible for it. And frankly, I'm rather surprised at you."

I pretended to study the toe of my high-tops. "Howie is a better player. Both Howie and Jennifer tried out, and Howie won."

"I understand that, dear, and I'm glad that you and Howie get along so well. But Jennifer has been on the team a long time, and I understand she's also a good player."

91

"She is," I agreed.

"However," my mother went on, "I have a strange feeling that she may have been passed over for that quarterback position because she's female—or because Howie is your cousin."

"I wanted Howie to be on the team because I thought it would be fun for us to have lots in common," I said.

"I can see your point, dear, but I don't like to see you abuse power that way. Try not to do that again." Then she walked out of the room.

The phone practically rang off the hook that evening with questions about Howie's arm. Everybody believed the story about the ligament strain.

"He's incredible," Josh said. "If I hurt my arm that badly, I probably wouldn't play for a month."

While we were getting ready for bed, Sharon called again about the uniforms. "Four of the girls offered to donate uniforms, and get this: Karen's mom is a beautician and she's going to donate some worn-out wigs."

"Out of sight!" Howie said when he heard the news. "Let's work on filling up our football."

I found a slightly deflated old football in

my closet. I selected the inner ingredients for it while Howie called Josh and Noah to tell them our plan.

I mixed the gunk together and dumped it into a plastic container half-filled with pickle juice. Our concoction was now perfected.

"Are you sure we shouldn't motorize the ball?" Howie asked before we went to bed.

"Naw, this will be enough," I assured him.

When we arrived at school Thursday morning, the upper school was filled with heavy-duty football spirit. SLASH THE SAMURAI and WALLOP THE WOLVERINES banners were plastered all over the walls. The sixth-grade boosters handed out Slaughter the Samurai buttons, and the seventh-grade boosters gave out Whip the Wolverines tags.

Sharon met us outside our classroom. "Here are the uniforms," she said. "Try not to get them dirty."

Noah, Josh, Howie and I put the uniforms on right before lunch. The wigs looked pretty silly so we put our helmets on over them.

At exactly sixteen minutes after twelve, the four of us marched into the cafeteria. Howie stood about forty feet from Oscar, with the ball in both hands.

We all yelled, "Special delivery for Oscar!"

Howie heaved the ball, and it sailed across

the cafeteria. It splashed right on Oscar's chest, the gunk oozing down his plaid shirt.

"Who did that?" he yelled and aimed a tuna salad sandwich at Noah.

Noah ducked and the sandwich hit an eighth-grade girl. She promptly hurled a plum across the room.

"You don't throw very well for a football player!" she screamed at him.

"Food fight! Food fight! Food fight!" Other kids started banging on their tables, and the whole place was up for grabs. The four of us hid under Sharon's table so we wouldn't get the girls' uniforms messed up, and so we wouldn't get caught.

For the next few minutes, sandwiches, fruit and yogurt containers went flying. Then Mrs. Riley stepped into the cafeteria.

"Who is responsible for this mess?" she asked.

She could not get a straight answer. Everybody was blaming somebody else. Few people realized we were the cause, and we tried to stifle our laughs as we watched from under the table.

"Very well," Mrs. Riley said. "Fifteen minutes' detention for everybody today. And don't try to sneak out. I've got a list of everybody who eats this period."

Everyone booed and groaned. I wasn't

thrilled about the detention, but all the Wolverines agreed it had been worth watching Oscar get zapped. Nobody traced the food fight to us, except for Oscar. I found a note in my locker the next day. "The Wolverines will look like this after Sunday." Glued to the note was a picture of a dead wolf.

By Friday evening, Howie was a minor celebrity. His name was in the "Kidbits" column in the local newspaper.

It's anyone's guess who will win Clifton's annual football event between the sixth- and seventh-graders.

The Seventh Grade Samurai appear more confident, but the Sixth Grade Wolverines' new quarterback, Howie Pentergasser, could challenge any team.

The spectacular running and passing ability he demonstrated at practice should keep the older guys on their toes.

"Do you think I should cut this article out and bring it to the party tomorrow night?" Howie asked.

"No, I'm sure everybody will have read it by then," I said.

EIGHT

My folks insisted on taking pictures of Howie and me before we left for Sharon's party.

"Smile," my mother said. "You both look *so* cute."

I had to admit that both Howie and I looked pretty good. Howie was wearing a pair of acid-washed denims and a green plaid button-down shirt. I was dressed in a pair of neatly pressed khakis and a light blue oxford shirt. Still, I didn't want a photo session.

"We've really got to get going," I told my mother. Howie and I headed toward the front door.

But then my father grabbed the camera. "Let your mother have a social history on you if she wants," he snapped.

I looked at Al, who was sitting on the sofa, studying logarithms and laughing at us in that hyenalike guffaw of his. "I bet you didn't take pictures of Al's social history in upper school," I said.

"Come to think of it, Al had no social events to take pictures of," my mother mused.

Howie and I burst out laughing. Al ignored us and went back to his homework.

"Let's get going." I practically pulled Howie out the door.

"Have fun!" my mother yelled. "And call us when you're ready to come home. I'd hate to see you and Howie walking home late. And make sure you introduce Howie to everyone."

"They are so embarrassing," I muttered to Howie as we walked to the corner.

"Tim, they don't have the same sort of memory file on Albert. Be fair," Howie said.

I thought about Al sitting on the sofa watching us leave. Al rarely had friends over or even got phone calls. I don't remember him ever going to a party. Although this was my first official boy-girl gathering, I'd always been invited to birthday parties. I love them. It's fun to eat, play games and get goodie bags. And I love to watch kids unwrap their presents. It gives me ideas on my future wants.

"Should we review party procedures again?" Howie asked for the umpteenth time.

"Just act real impressed with everything. Don't complain if you don't like the food, and thank Sharon's mother when we leave. And make sure if you dance with any girls, that you don't get too close."

"Do you think we'll play spin-the-bottle or seven minutes in heaven?" Howie asked excitedly.

"Howie, I can't believe that Al programmed those ideas into you!"

"He didn't. Josh and Neil talked about it yesterday when we changed into our uniforms. It sounds like fun." Howie smiled and his blue eyes lit up.

"No, Howie, I doubt if we'll play kissing games. Sharon's mother and father will probably be around," I said.

I wondered what we might be doing at Sharon's. I figured we'd probably dance and listen to records. Personally, I thought kissing games might be fun, but I would never admit that to Howie. As we neared Sharon's house I noticed a SLAUGHTER THE SAMURAI banner on her front lawn.

The moment we got to her house, Howie

rummaged in his pocket and took out a small gift-wrapped box.

"What is that?" I asked Howie.

"A present for the party girl," he said.

"It's not Sharon's birthday. I thought you knew that. Put it back."

"I know it's not her birthday," Howie answered. "But I can give it to her, anyway."

"No you can't," I argued. "She'll think you like her. Put it back now." I rang the doorbell and hoped Howie would follow my advice.

"But I do like her. She invited me to a party. I like people who are nice to me," Howie insisted.

"You don't give presents to people you barely know. Especially if they're female. What's in there, anyway?" I asked.

"A necklace," he announced.

Howie had me baffled this time. I know jewelry is expensive and I couldn't quite figure how he could have afforded it. "How did you pay for it?" I asked.

"I didn't."

"You mean you stole it? I'm taking you home and switching you off," I threatened him.

"I didn't steal it." Howie sounded hurt. "I made it out of a big microchip and carved an S on it with a screwdriver."

I was sorry I'd asked, and I couldn't argue with Howie any longer. Mrs. Rawson came to the door and greeted us. We followed her into the house. I wished that Howie had not been invited and could have stayed home.

Mrs. Rawson looked a little like Sharon, with blue eyes and black hair. "It looks like you've really grown, Timmy." She studied Howie. "So, this is your cousin whom I've heard so much about. I loved that article in the paper. Sharon tells me you're smart, too."

"Thank you," Howie answered, looking around the living room. "This is a beautiful home. And you look just like your daughter."

Mrs. Rawson smiled at Howie. "Sharon was right about you being a nice boy. Tim is lucky to have a cousin like you."

I heard the party noises in the basement and quickly fled downstairs. Howie was making me sick to my stomach, but I felt even worse when I joined the party. On a card table by the stairs there was a small pile of presents. The givers must have mistakenly thought it was Sharon's birthday, or, like Howie, were being extra nice. Howie came down to the basement a minute later.

"This is so sweet of you, Howie." Sharon touched his arm when he placed his gift on the table. "It's not my birthday, but I'll open my gifts later."

I was just glad she didn't kiss him on the cheek.

I hoped we'd leave before the unwrapping session, or maybe Howie's gift would get misplaced. Everybody would think he was nuts giving a girl a necklace made of a microchip.

Sharon had invited a lot of people. Most of the kids involved with the football team had been invited, plus a bunch of kids from our class. There were even a few kids that didn't go to our school.

It was almost like two separate parties. The boys stood on one side of the room stuffing their mouths with pizza, pretzels and hot dogs. The girls didn't eat anything. They drank soda and they looked like they were comparing outfits and checking the guys out. Instead of the usual jeans and jogging suits, all the girls were wearing dresses or miniskirts.

Neil came up to me and punched me lightly on the arm. "How's it going? I can't wait for that game tomorrow." He pointed to Howie and put his hand on his shoulder, "So, how is the kid that's going to win the game for us?"

"Mega-terrific," Howie answered.

A bunch of kids crowded around us.

"Hey," Neil motioned to one of the kids I didn't know to come over to us. "This is Milt from Boone." Neil put his hand on Howie's shoulder. "This is Tim Watkins and his cousin Howie. Howie is our quarterback and an ace player. You better watch out if we ever play Boone."

"Glad to meet you two," Milt said. "Do you play, Tim?"

"Yeah," I answered weakly. It seemed like nobody cared that I was captain anymore, or the one who had found Howie for the team.

I strode around the room, keeping my eye on Howie. He definitely did not need me to introduce him to anybody. He did a good job of it himself. I wondered if Al had programmed a magnet into Howie that attracted people to him.

Sharon made an announcement after everybody arrived. "I know that most of us are familiar with each other, but I want to make sure we *all* know each other." First she introduced the kids from the other schools. Lastly she presented Howie.

Everybody waved their hands in the air and started yelling stuff like, "Power to Pentergasser!" One of the girls I didn't know had seen his picture in the paper and wanted his autograph.

When Sharon turned on some records, we

all started dancing. Every girl wanted to dance with Howie. I danced one number with Susi and another with Sharon. I considered asking Jennifer to dance, but she was taller than me and I thought she might still be sore about the quarterback business. I now wondered if it might have been better to have chosen her for the job.

After we finished dancing, Sharon made an announcement.

"The person who guesses the closest number to the amount of jelly beans in that jar on the table wins all of them." She placed a box with a slit in it by the huge jar. "Put your answers in this box with your name on them."

Everybody made a beeline for the candy and started guessing.

"I guess that there's a million." Josh put his answer into the box.

I guessed one hundred thousand and thirty-six. I really wanted those jelly beans. They were the gourmet kind, in exotic flavors like watermelon, coconut and root beer.

Howie observed the jar carefully. He picked it up and shook it gently. Listening closely, I could hear a mild buzz coming from Howie's math co-processor like a printer running a page off. He wrote down the number 9,386 in that neat handwriting he has.

Then I noticed Howie nod his head and yawn. Quickly I attempted to drag him into the bathroom. Everyone looked at us strangely. "I need to talk to you a minute, Howie," I said, "in private."

Howie stretched his arms over his head and yawned again. He looked annoyed.

I put my arm on his shoulder and managed to pull him away.

"Hey, what are you trying to do?" Howie asked when I shut the door to the bathroom.

"I need to change your battery." I looked inside my pocket. It was empty. "Oh, no. We're in big trouble. I forgot your battery, and if we don't leave you'll have a fainting spell."

"How could you forget something that important?" Howie asked.

"I didn't exactly forget," I told him. "I didn't put them in my pocket when I changed pants."

"I was having a terrific time and you totally ruined it. I bet you did this on purpose!" Howie said.

"I did not!" I protested.

"Prove it by letting me stay longer."

"I can't, Howie."

"You're just jealous because I'm the life of the party," Howie said.

I crossed my arms over my chest and stared

at him. How could you argue with an android, anyway? I wondered. "I'm giving you a choice, Howie. You can embarrass yourself and conk out in front of everybody and ruin everything, or we can leave now."

Howie frowned at me, and then the two of us went back to the party.

"I think Howie ate something that didn't agree with him," I told everybody. "We have to go home."

Both Sharon and her mother expressed extreme interest and followed us upstairs.

"You looked fine before," Mrs. Rawson said. "But I know there's a flu bug that's been going around lately." She put her hand on Howie's forehead. "Funny. You don't *feel* warm."

After I made the call, I stood by the door and waited for my father. We rushed Howie into the van as soon as he arrived.

Al was sitting in the front with my dad. "You've got to be more careful with those batteries, Tim," he said. "You can't forget them. One more incident like this and I'm going to recreate Howie to be a kid *my* age."

"Yeah," Howie said sleepily. "I wanted to play spin-the-bottle with Sharon."

"Cut it out, Howie, or I just might not put any batteries in you at all!" I was getting so

106

sick of hearing about how much he liked Sharon.

The second we got Howie home, I replaced all of his batteries to make sure he'd be okay for the game tomorrow. Al took Howie in the basement to tune up his waterproof backup subsystem. The weather prediction was possible rain.

About ten-thirty in the evening, Sharon called and asked for Howie. "He's sleeping," I told her.

"Do you think he'll make it to the game?"

"Yeah," I said. "It was an upset stomach, like I told you."

"I'm so glad he doesn't have the flu. By the way, give Howie this message." Sharon paused for a moment. "Howie won the jelly beans. He guessed the number exactly! Can you believe it? My mother will drop the jar off when she drives a few of the kids home."

"He'll be happy about that," I answered. I guessed she'd be opening her gifts later.

"And," Sharon went on, "tell him I just *love* his present. I'm wearing it to the game tomorrow for good luck."

"Yeah. I'll tell him," I said. "Good night." I hung up the phone and sighed.

NINE

I don't believe in horoscopes, numerology or Tarot cards like my folks do. But I have a thing about the weather. If it's bright and sunny I'm confident that the day will go smoothly. If it's cloudy I get bad vibes.

Sunday morning was the sort of day that could have gone either way. The clouds kept moving in and out.

Howie leaped out of bed in great spirits. "At this time tomorrow we'll be the champs at Clifton!" he announced.

I threw a pillow at him. "It's not good to be overly confident.

"I'd call it realistic." Howie blew on his fingers and rubbed them on his pajama top.

I looked at the clock. It was 9:05—only four

hours until we had to be at the field for warm-ups. Only five hours until the game.

All morning Howie and I practiced passing and kicking in the backyard, while Al watched to make sure Howie worked without glitches. A short period of drizzle scared me, but it didn't seem to affect Howie or bother Al.

"You sure this weather won't mess you up?" I asked Howie.

"Don't be a turkey," Howie answered. "Haven't I caught every pass you've thrown today?"

"He's right," Al assured me. "Howie is now one hundred percent waterproof. And according to my calculations of barometric pressure and humidity density, we'll only have light drizzle today."

I looked at the sky dubiously, but I figured Al would know. He's hardly ever wrong about scientific stuff.

"By the way," Al said. "Mom, Dad and I will be sitting on a bench toward the front today, in case there's any problem. Did you remember the batteries?"

"Of course I did," I answered, remembering last night's fiasco. Thank goodness that had happened yesterday so we'd be prepared for today.

When Howie and I got to the field, we felt

almost like professional players. Loudspeakers had been set up by the back of the stands, and I could hear the school band tuning up. Majorettes twirled their batons to the school fight song.

Win for our team.
Win for our team.
Get that ball and fight. Sportsmanship is your first name,
So win with all your might. Fight! Fight! Fight!

Although it was an hour until game time, spectators had already arrived, and the eighth-grade boosters were selling programs. Frankie's had a refreshment wagon on the south end of the park.

"Wow, this is really something," Howie told me, looking at a program. "Our names are in here."

"Let me see." And sure enough, the whole team was listed. I looked at my name and Howie's a few times.

Timothy Watkins	*Fullback*	*90 lbs.*
Howard Pentergasser	*Quarterback*	*93 lbs.*

Some fifth-grade girls waved at us, but our glory was quickly interrupted by Oscar Novotny, who blocked our way onto the field.

Oscar held up the newspaper article with Howie's name in it. "You think you're so great, Pentergasser? You won't after today." Oscar tore up the article and let the pieces fall to the ground. Then he pressed them into the dirt with his shoe. "We'll run through you so fast that you won't be any better off than a pile of mud. See you on the field." Then he ran over to the south end of the park for the Samurai pregame warm-ups.

In spite of Oscar's threat, I felt confident during our exercises. Everybody seemed to be in top shape, including Howie—even though the drizzle had resumed. Howie didn't even fumble when Neil tossed him a difficult lateral pass.

By game time there was a huge crowd. Kids from kindergarten through eighth grade jammed the benches along with several parents. I saw Al and my parents sitting near the front, as they had promised.

A few minutes before the game, an announcement came over the loudspeaker. "Welcome to the challenge between the Sixth Grade Wolverines and the Seventh Grade Samurai. It ought to be an exciting demonstration of skills today between two junior

111

teams that have practiced diligently over the summer. . . ."

We sang the "Star Spangled Banner," the whistle shrilled and the game began.

"Since the Wolverines are the youngest, they get to choose on the toss," the referee told us. "Heads or tails?" he asked as he flipped the coin.

"Tails!" I hollered.

We won the toss.

"Howie, you call it," I said, thinking Howie would like to be involved.

"We'll kick off!" Howie yelled.

"What?" Noah look astonished. "Nobody kicks off when they win the toss."

"Where is your head?" Neil asked. "Once they get the ball, they'll keep it."

"Are you *sure* this is what you want to do?" Josh asked.

"Of course, I'm sure." Howie shook his head and looked at us like we were complete idiots. "They'll fumble it and we'll get it back from them. According to the prevailing weather conditions of a muddy field and damp air, the Samurai will not have the ball for long. I guarantee you," he said confidently.

"I suppose we can give it a try," I agreed, unsure of Howie's idea. I hated arguing with my cousin in front of everybody.

"Let's get going," the referee shouted, "or you'll be penalized for delay of the game!"

The crowd watched curiously. There was a hum of conversation. Some fans booed and hissed. The ball was placed on the tee. Josh signaled he was ready, the whistle blew and Josh kicked the ball out of bounds.

"In a rather unusual start, the Wolverines have kicked the ball out of bounds," the announcer said.

After we moved five yards back, Josh kicked again, and the ball soared through the air. The wind took it all the way to the Samurai end zone. Norm Bellini caught it and ran to the twenty-yard line before being tackled.

We got into a huddle and it began to drizzle harder. "We've got to get that ball," I said.

"How about a DD Ninety-Eight Point Three?" Howie suggested.

"That's an offensive play and we're on defense, if you hadn't noticed!" Noah growled.

"Lets try to trap them," Jennifer suggested. "Maybe we can bring the carrier down."

The whistle interrupted us.

"Too long in the huddle! You're penalized five yards."

"Let's get going!" Howie shouted. "Uno, dos, tres."

"What's he doing?" Noah asked me. "We don't have any signals in Spanish."

"I don't know," I answered. I wondered why Howie was acting so spacy. Al had assured me that Howie could not be ruined by the rain.

"Let's get that ball," Jennifer called out.

With all my strength I knocked Oscar over, and Norm stripped the ball out of Oscar's hands. Jennifer snatched it off the ground and ran five yards before being brought down.

Later I gained ten yards, but one of the Samurai linebackers caught me by the ankles, bringing me to the ground. By the end of the quarter the Samurai had made a touchdown. We were all covered with mud and grass.

I hoped that changing goals might change our luck. It didn't. The drizzle turned to rain. The Samurai hung on to the ball until Howie intercepted a high, spiraling pass intended for Oscar, and ran with it, nearing the Samurai forty-yard line.

The Wolverines fans went wild.

Howie was almost tackled by three players, but he dodged them and kept slogging down the muddy field.

"Good going," Coach Rumbaugh yelled.

The cheerleaders threw their pompons into

the air. "Power to Pentergasser!" they shouted in unison.

Then Howie turned around and started running in the opposite direction, toward our end zone.

"That's the wrong way, you idiot!" I hollered.

We all ran after him, but we couldn't stop him. Howie scored a touchdown—for the Samurai.

At the end of the first half, the score was Wolverines 0, Samurai 14.

TEN

"I told you Howie was a spy," Susi yelled.

"Yeah," Noah said. "Next he's going to start eating lunch with Oscar Novotny and sleeping over at his house."

Then everybody shouted accusations at both of us. Susi even thought Howie and I were running a betting pool with the Samurai, and purposely throwing the game off.

I was glad when the coach came over and calmed us down.

"What's going on here, Howie?" he asked Howie while we walked off the field for half-time break.

"I—I got mixed up when we changed goals."

"And why did you want to start off by kicking?" Coach Rumbaugh persisted.

"Well, I thought we could use some experimental plays today."

"You *what?*" the coach snarled. "This is the big game—not practice."

"If you want to do experiments, try them in the science lab," Susi snapped.

"I'm sorry. I thought the kickoff strategy would work," Howie said.

Coach Rumbaugh looked at Howie sadly. "I guess some kids just don't perform well under pressure. I'm sorry, Howard, but I can't have you play as quarterback. Tim, choose somebody else."

"I'll do it, Timmy!" Josh volunteered.

"No, I think we have somebody better." I pointed to Jennifer. "Howie can take her place."

Then Howie and I made a beeline for the benches, where Al was waiting.

I pulled Al over. "Come into the locker room with us. I thought you told me that Howie was waterproofed!"

"He is," Al assured me. "I bet you didn't put in the batteries right. How come you're always so careless?"

"I am not careless," I told him. "He worked fine this morning."

Al and I continued to argue until we got into the locker room, where Mr. Know It All found that the batteries were in correctly.

"Maybe they are defective," Al mused. "I'm writing a nasty letter to Discount Electronics," he said, handing me a new set from his pocket.

Quickly, I inserted them into Howie's battery chamber, and we ran back out onto the field.

I felt more optimistic when the second half of the game began. The rain had stopped but the field was still muddy. The Samurai kicked off and Howie signaled for it. I prayed that he wouldn't mess up this time—for both our sakes.

Howie caught the ball safely and made it to the twenty-five-yard line before being toppled.

"Good try!" Josh told him.

But as hard as we tried, we couldn't get a first down. Six minutes into the third quarter, the Samurai had the ball on our thirty-five-yard line, and they were creeping forward fast.

"Rattrap," Jennifer called out as Norm, ball in hand, tried to zigzag over the field. Howie tackled him before he could gain any yardage.

"Wow," everybody said.

A few minutes later, Norm clipped Josh and got a fifteen-yard penalty. They had to punt, and we got the ball back.

With only three minutes left in the third quarter, Jennifer took the snap from Josh and just started running as fast as she could, with Oscar in hot pursuit. But she was lighter and faster and kept well ahead of him. Oscar couldn't catch up with her, and she crossed the goal line. Coach Rumbaugh still let Howie try the extra point, even though he had messed up as quarterback. I heaved a sigh of relief when the ball sailed, through the uprights—a little low, but it would do.

The scoreboard lit up; it was now 14–7, and the Samurai were furious. The Wolverines' fans went wild, and I saw Jennifer's folks hug each other.

"Can't you even catch a girl?" I overheard Norm say to Oscar.

At the beginning of the fourth quarter, Jennifer passed me the ball and I ran eighteen yards for our second touchdown. Howie made the extra point again, and the score was now tied.

With thirty seconds left in the game, the ball was seventeen yards from the Samurai goal line. All we needed to win was a field goal.

We all looked at Howie. He was the only one who could kick it that well. He smiled, and a minute later kicked the ball smoothly over the crossbars.

The Wolverines' fans jumped up and down in the benches.

I hugged Jennifer. Jennifer hugged me and Howie. Then she kissed us both on the cheek.

"The two teams will now shake," the referee ordered.

We all got in line, and the first person I had to shake hands with was Oscar himself. He was not in a sporting mood.

"You think you guys are so great," he whispered in my ear. "Just watch your step, because I'm not through with you *or* your sleazeball cousin yet."

"Incredible playing," Howie said when we got home. The two of us were now sprawled on the sofa with our feet on the coffee table.

"Who do you two think you are?" Al asked angrily. "Mom will kill you if she sees your smelly feet on that antique table."

"We think we're winners, and we are," Howie joked.

"Yeah." I laughed, getting up and slapping Al on the back. "I bet the Samurai never got beat by a computer before. In a way you beat them, Al."

Howie and I both thought that was a riot. We burst into hysterics while Al scowled at us. Then he left the room. I wasn't sure if he was angry, or whether he just thought we were crazy.

"Hey, what happened to you in the first half, anyway?" I asked Howie.

He shrugged. "Well, let's put it this way. The rain dampened my brain."

"Wait a minute, kiddo. I thought that you were well waterproofed. And I'm sure those batteries were in right," I told him.

Howie grinned. "That Jennifer is a good quarterback, isn't she?" He patted me on the back. "You don't do so bad yourself. I don't know, maybe the batteries were defective."

I began to think about Howie's performance today. Why *had* he played so crazily for that short while?

"Did you act insane on purpose?" I asked him.

An electronic buzz came out of Howie. "Processing system cannot answer due to nature of question," he said in a computerlike voice.

"C'mon, Howie, tell me!" I pleaded.

He ignored my question. From under the sofa he pulled out two emptied mayonnaise jars now filled with gourmet jelly beans. He handed a jar to me.

"There's four thousand, six hundred ninety-three jelly beans for you, and four thousand, six hundred ninety-three jelly beans for me," he said.

"What's this for?" I asked.

"I thought if I gave you an equal share of the prize it might even the score between us. I sorted the candy so we'd have the same amount."

"Thanks, Howie," I said.

We clinked our jars of gourmet jelly beans together as if we were toasting each other, and tossed some into our mouths.

I watched Howie chew for a minute. "Hey, I thought you weren't supposed to eat when you were at home," I told him. I eyed his jar of jelly beans. "I'll trade you for some delicious, fresh batteries," I said.

"No way!" Howie exclaimed.

Then we both burst out laughing.

For more way-out adventures of the All-American Android, be sure to read THE HALLOWEEN HEX, the next book in the HIGH-TECH HOWARD series!

Tim and his android "cousin" Howie are both looking forward to Halloween. There's going to be a big party at school, with prizes for the best costume, and after that, they're both planning a trip to the Warren house—the neighborhood's spookiest residence.

Everything would be just fine, if it wasn't for Oscar Novotny, the seventh-grade bully who keeps threatening to beat them up. To prevent Oscar from ruining their Halloween fun, Tim and Howie do things to make him think there's a witch in town who has put a hex on him. Oscar is just dumb enough (and superstitious enough) to believe it—at first.

But when Oscar discovers he's been tricked, he sets out to get revenge, and the "treat" he plans for Howie and Tim makes this the scariest Halloween ever!